# House of Hearts

*Veronika Sophia Robinson*

Sweet Cinnamon
*Romance*

*You're not rich until you
have something money can't buy.*

# About Veronika Sophia Robinson

Veronika spent her childhood on a 700-acre horse stud in rural Australia, and her teenage years immersed in romance novels. They provided just the antidote to boring school days and tedious exams. Instead of doing homework, she was being romanced by tall, dark, fictional men...that is, until she could hear her mother walking up the hallway to her bedroom. And then, her secret lover was shoved beneath her textbooks while she pretended to studiously examine the theory of how to dissect a frog. Talk about going from princes to frogs! She was thrown out of biology class for drawing hearts. Love hearts!

She met her husband Paul—a prince, not a frog—when living in New Zealand, and they moved in together the day after their first date. It was 'I've known you forever' at first sight. Their love story is a rom-com; she's the rom, he's the com. Veronika has been a marriage celebrant since 1995, when her first daughter just started kicking inside her belly.

She lives a charmed life in the heart of the Cumbrian countryside, in the north of England.

Veronika's passions include barefoot gardening, plant-based cooking, psychological astrology, reading and writing, walking in the woods, and being with her family and friends. www.veronikarobinson.com

**House Of Hearts**
© Veronika Sophia Robinson
© Cover illustration by Heidi Harbers
Published by Sweet Cinnamon Romance
An imprint of Starflower Press
ISBN: 978-0-9931586-8-1
St. Valentine's Day 2023

A CIP catalogue record for this book is available from the British Library.

Published by Sweet Cinnamon Romance, an imprint of Starflower Press www.starflowerpress.com


Books by the same author at www.veronikarobinson.com

*Sweet Cinnamon Romances*
*are contemporary love stories set around the world.*
*Cinnamon symbolises abundance, protection and passion.*

# The Mystery

'So, Simon, this is a pretty big step, isn't it? Six months leave from this newspaper and TV presenting to write your next book. I can't wait to read it.'

'Thanks, Frank. I've written most of it already, and I'm rather pleased with it, but it is missing something. One more chapter should do it. I need another business to focus on, and it will be a lot easier to do while I'm on sabbatical. I get so caught up in writing deadlines and filming the breakfast show that I lose my focus on the book.'

Frank passed him a bottle of vintage champagne. 'You're the best financial journalist we've ever had working on this paper. You sure will leave a hole behind.'

Frank's personal assistant, Gemma, walked in with a large hamper. 'This is from all of us, Simon. We're really going to miss you!' She reached over and pecked him on the cheek. For five years she'd been trying to get his attention, but for one reason or another he never seemed interested.

'Simon was just saying he needs to include another business to profile in his book. Any ideas, Gemma? You, of all people, have more contacts than all of us put together. There must be a recession-proof business that Simon could write about. Something a bit different, to make his book stand out? What do you think?'

'No, sorry,' she said, walking away, hoping Simon would see how long her legs looked in the killer high heels she was wearing. He didn't.

'Actually' she said, turning around, 'if you were prepared to step out of your comfort zone, Simon, I reckon I know the perfect place.'

Simon ran his fingers through his dark, slightly wavy hair, trying to suppress a smile. Gemma always was the oddball in the office. What was she going to suggest?

'House of Hearts. As far as I know, it hasn't been featured in any magazines or newspapers or television, and yet it's a thriving venture. It would be perfect for your book, and probably wake up all those hard-nosed business men who hang off your every word.' Gemma began walking away again, and then turned around with a laugh. 'I'll bet you haven't featured any businesses owned by women, have you? *Have you!*'

Simon felt the colour rise to his cheeks, and was grateful that he'd not taken the time to shave for the past two mornings.

'Guilty as charged, Gemma. Okay, so what is this House of Hearts, and where is it?' he asked good-humouredly, with no intention of following it up. Of course he couldn't! He'd be the laughing stock of the financial-news industry.

'Simon Beaudin, if you're going to feature it in your book, you have to visit. This isn't something you can do over the internet or by phone interview. You have to experience House of Hearts.'

'Gemma, I have to be honest: the name alone is making me feel nauseas. Seriously? House of Hearts. Come on. This is a joke, right?'

'Your loss,' she said, smiling, and walked out of the office.

'Aren't you at least going to look it up?' Frank asked.

'You're kidding, right?' Simon chuckled, taking the last sip of his now-cold espresso.

'Your choice, but Gemma knows her stuff. Don't

dismiss her as just my PA or presume that a small business isn't worth mentioning. It would give the book a unique selling point.'

Simon bade farewell, and drove through the busy New York streets with the words 'House of Hearts' never leaving his consciousness. Mildly irritated, he pulled into the plaza basement and passed his keys to the concierge.

Fetching his brief case and box of notes from the boot, he then took the elevator to the top floor. As it opened to his penthouse, he laughed: definitely *not* a house of hearts, whatever that was. No, his home was modern and sleek, with views across the city and river. Simon had earned his life of luxury with years of toil, finally building a reputation as the go-to man for anything financial. A funny sensation gripped him mid-belly and involuntarily forced his ripped abdominal muscles to twitch. 'Don't be silly,' he said out loud. 'Stick with your House of Money!'

Filling the kettle for his sixth coffee of the day, he then switched on the news in time for the financial report he'd recorded earlier. This was his daily ritual. Home from the office by eight, watch the news, write up articles, listen to a little late night jazz, sip a glass of Irish Whiskey, then go to bed. He'd wake early and then drive to the TV station to film the 6am financial segment.

Simon Beaudin had worked hard to reach the pinnacle of his career, and he felt a smug satisfaction at the enviable lifestyle he'd created for himself.

When he awoke the following morning, his eyes weren't even open when the words 'House of Hearts' tinkled like sleigh bells in his ears.

'Good Lord, no!'

Simon hit the shower, trying to wash the words away.

This morning there was no commute through the city to the TV recording studios. Today was the first day of his sabbatical, and he intended to get straight into the business of writing. The study was a perfect place to work, with views over the Hudson River, but why did he feel so distracted? Where was his sense of discipline? Perhaps he shouldn't have had that second glass of whiskey last night?

Simon typed 'House of Hearts' into the internet search engine. That's odd, he thought to himself. No web address? How can a thriving business not have a web address? Maybe Gemma had been winding him up. Any minute now, he was going to phone her and give her a piece of his mind! Then he noticed personal blogs for pages and pages through the search engine coming up with references to House of Hearts: best honeymoon ever; mind-blowing food; perfect gingerbread hearts, couldn't eat enough of them; Soraya was the perfect hostess; a piece of magic; heaven; the best massage I've ever had; Soraya knows a thing or two about love; the hot tub under the stars on the night of our honeymoon was the icing on the cake; and so it went on.

He searched *Soraya Juniper*.

*Marriage Celebrant. Soraya has been officiating wedding ceremonies since she was 21 years old, and is in demand for couples seeking the ideal intimate wedding.*

Simon was surprised that there wasn't a photo with her profile, nor was there any mention of her association with House of Hearts. The whole thing seemed rather odd; mysterious, even. There weren't even any contact details. Yes, odd. Maybe Gemma didn't mention this place after all, and he really did have too much to drink last night?

Simon switched off the internet, which he always did when he wanted to focus on his writing, but the next few hours were anything but focused. After his third cup of coffee, Simon reluctantly phoned Gemma.

'So, where is this House of Hearts?' and he cursed slightly as he heard her muffled squeal of delight.

'Rainbow Valley,' she said, and he could almost feel her smile coming down the phone line.

'You're joking, right?'

'Not at all. It's truly a magical place. One of the eight wonders of the world, if you ask me.'

'Gemma, I've tried searching online for House of Hearts, and there's no website.'

'That's right. It's all word of mouth.'

'In this day and age?' Simon shook his head in disbelief. 'You're pulling my leg, right?'

'I know it doesn't make sense, but trust me on this Simon. Please. You won't regret it, and I dare say: it might just change your life.'

Simon raised his eyebrows, and thanked her for her time. 'Do you have a phone number for House of Hearts?'

'Simon, the shop doesn't have a phone. Soraya says it disturbs the ambience. She does her business by face to face or via letter. You know, pen and paper? The old-fashioned way?'

Was that mockery slithering down the phone line, he wondered.

'You are *kidding* me! Gemma, this isn't some practical joke is it? You're not sending me on a wild-goose chase as payback for not asking you out?'

'Simon! Of course not! I've got an album full of

photos of Rainbow Valley and House of Hearts. Why don't you come over sometime and see them?'

After he declined her offer, Simon searched for Rainbow Valley.

'At least that exists,' he said to himself when links came up on the search engine.

After twenty minutes of reading, he concluded that this off-the-beaten-track small town did appear rather quaint and magical, but he couldn't help wonder why House of Hearts wasn't mentioned on the town's website, despite there being links to thirty other businesses in the area. Once again, he shook his head in disbelief.

'You're crazy, Simon. Crazy!' he said to himself, and headed to the master suite to pack a suitcase, figuring that he might as well go up there for a few days before completing the book. And, he hoped, he could erase the words 'House of Hearts' from his mind once and for all.

# The Heart's A Funny Thing

Soraya sang along to *The Heart*, an old country-music song by Larry Gatlin which was playing on the radio; and then she transitioned to a hum when the first customer of the day entered her shop.

'Good morning Marjorie. How are you today?' she said.

'Just fine my love, just fine.' Marjorie, a sprightly 76-year-old woman with long silver braids to her bottom, had left her bicycle on the front verandah of House of Hearts, and came in for her morning gingerbread. This was her daily habit, not dissimilar to most people in the small town of Rainbow Valley. House of Hearts, despite being at the very end of the main street, was, in fact, the centre of town. It was the heartbeat of the valley; the place where folks gathered to chat and catch up on news.

'They sure smell good this morning,' she said enthusiastically, taking the first bite of the heart-shaped cookie.

Soraya smiled. This was often her favourite time of day. When her doors opened at 10am, people were drawn in by the aroma of ginger, cloves, nutmeg, cinnamon, almonds, and honey.

'You really should charge us for eating these. How many dozen do you make each morning?' Marjorie asked.

'About fifteen dozen,' Soraya said brightly, 'But you know as well as I do that most people take a handful when they come by, rather than just one. I don't mind though. It's such a lovely way to start the day.'

'I've baked your recipe more than a dozen times, but I have to tell you Soraya, they never taste as good as the ones you make. Mine are good, but these are delicious. What is the difference? What didn't you write on the recipe sheet?'

'Marjorie, I swear, every ingredient is mentioned.' Soraya batted her eyelids in mock shock, and placed her hand over her heart, but they both smiled at the truth: there *was* an ingredient she failed to mention.

They laughed and made small talk as other people came in, grabbed their cookies, and headed back to work. Jess Jasonille popped by for her cookie while delivering eggs to the elderly folk around town.

'Jess, I can't believe you're still wearing those jeans,' Soraya laughed, taking in the sight of the huge ripped knee area. Pop upstairs to my bedroom and wrap my dressing gown around yourself, then bring those jeans back here,' she said, trying to sound bossy and mother-like. 'You're not leaving here till I've mended them!'

Marjorie laughed, then headed out of the shop. Jess did as she was told, and then Soraya got to work rummaging through her bag of scrap fabric until she came across a lovely piece of fine corduroy in maroon. She cut a heart shape, the size of her hand, then carefully stitched it into place. And this was how most of her work days went. People popped by for cookies or mending or simply to sit and chat with Soraya about whatever was happening around town. Many of the locals still bought hearts from her shop, but the majority of sales came from tourists passing through the quaint township. They often found themselves drawn into the shop, and unable to leave. House of Hearts had a magnetic aura that drew people in from the street. Curiosity brought them inside, and satisfaction walked with them, hand in hand, out of the door.

Jess left the shop, a pocket full of cookies taken hostage in her coat, and skipped down the street.

Soraya had a skip in her step, too, and gave thanks for another ordinary day. The days were loved as much as the fresh country air she breathed and the stars which hung low in the sky each night. Ordinary days, she thought, were extraordinary. She briefly scanned her to-do list for the day, and continued singing the song from earlier.

While the shop was quiet for a moment, she popped up two flights of stairs to her kitchen, and brought down another basket of cookies fresh from the oven. Soraya breathed in the aroma. Freshly grated organic lemon zest, just a smidgen, was the ingredient she 'forgot' to put on the recipe she handed out so freely.

Simon adjusted his tie as he slowed down by the bridge just before the small town. For some reason he couldn't explain, he found himself feeling a tad nervous. 'Don't be stupid,' he chastened, 'she's a business owner like any other. This isn't going to be harder than walking into the boardroom of a multinational and grilling CEOs. Get a grip!'

As his black soft-topped Audi purred over the arched sandstone bridge, he nearly choked when he read the sign on the other side. There, beneath an old oak, was the town's welcome sign: *Rainbow Valley: where you can find your pot of gold.*

'Good lord!' he said, half expecting fairies and goblins to come a-dancing out of the surrounding woodland. Simon stopped the car on the side of the road, and headed back to the bridge by foot. He needed fresh air. Clearly he'd been in the car way too long.

There was something magical about the shallow river, and the way the pebbles on the bottom sparkled in the sunlight. But wasn't every untouched place in nature just as charming? Just as beautiful? Simon breathed deeply, gathering his thoughts. Normally when he approached an interviewee, there were dozens of questions he'd penned, ready to pounce and tear his victim to shreds. This was what he did. This was his life's work. No wonder he felt out of place in a valley which purported to offer him a pot of gold. But maybe it was literal? *Maybe I'll earn my fortune here,* he laughed.

Coffee. Motel. House of Hearts. In that order. He repeated it like a mantra as he headed to the comfort of his car. Wealth. He loved how it smelt, and how it made him feel. *Just a quick interview, and then I'm out of here.*

The small town of Rainbow Valley was, much to his surprise, rather delightful, and far more enchanting than any of the photos on the town's website. Perhaps they didn't want to attract tourists, after all. Almost all of the businesses were in old wooden buildings, even the motel. Coffee first, he reminded himself, looking out for a coffee shop or Starbucks. He laughed at the thought of any chain store being welcomed here. *More chance of winning lotto,* he chuckled.

By the time he approached the far end of the street, it occurred to him that there wasn't a coffee shop in the town. 'You have got to be kidding!' he slapped his hand against the steering wheel. 'How do these people start their day?' Simon kept driving, looking for a place to turn around and search again for coffee, when he suddenly spied his destination at the end of the main street. There, perched like a tiny doll's house, was a building too cute to be anywhere other than in a romance novel. He didn't need the sign out front to tell him it was House of Hearts. Simon sat in the driver's seat for some time, taking in the building, and wondering about the woman who made a living from selling love hearts.

Reality hit him, and he put the gear into reverse, and was about to restart the engine. What on Earth had he been thinking? It was a stupid idea to include a business like this in his book. Stupid! Love hearts? What a fool! Gemma would be having a good laugh at his idiocy.

The four-story wooden house looked, despite being old, to be well cared for. He wondered if all four floors were retail space, or if perhaps Soraya lived upstairs. He'd soon find out, if he actually made up his mind to go in; but why the hell were his hands gripping the steering wheel so tightly? Simon noticed that his white knuckles soon pinked up as he let go and stepped out of the car. Fresh air. *Breathe,* he told himself. Simon gave himself a minute to breathe in the country air, noting that he was so far out of his comfort zone it wasn't funny.

The bottom floor of House of Hearts was about three feet off ground level, nestled on stilts, entered by a set of wide stairs, and surrounded by a spacious wooden verandah without railings. The blue building sat beautifully against the rich green of the surrounding woodland to the rear.

On the front door was an embedded stained-glass red love heart. The wooden window shutters, on the first three floors, had hearts carved into them. The second floor had a balcony around three sides. The attic window was the only thing normal about the place.

Simon wondered what the house would sell for on the open market. Would anyone actually buy a place which paid homage to affairs of the heart? Love wasn't something he gave much thought to. After all, his friends married years ago, and look how miserable they were. Most were heading for the divorce courts, and those who decided to stick it out 'because of the children' were spending more time away from home than there. Even his own parents divorced when he was a teenager. Love, what a joke! And here he was about to interview someone who clearly believed in it enough to make a business out of it. *A recession-proof business*, he reminded himself. That's the only reason he was here. To make money. Money from his book. Not to find a pot of gold. Not to be enchanted. And *not* to feel love.

And then, all of a sudden, he wondered about Soraya's husband, and what he made of all this fluffy love stuff. Maybe he was just as off this planet as she appeared to be. *No website!*

Simon shook his head and headed up to the shop.

What was that smell? Whatever it was, it made him even more desperate for coffee. Without meaning to be led astray, he followed the tantalising aroma, and found it was coming from House of Hearts.

'You're not getting to my heart through my stomach,' he laughed as he took the steps up onto the verandah.

There was an old porch swing with cushions in love-heart fabric. Of course. The door mat was heart-shaped. Of course. Simon felt his heart sinking, and his last thought was: *Gemma, you'll pay for this!*

There was a tinkle of the string of heart-shaped bells as he pushed the door open, and then the scent of ginger and cloves whooshed at him, making him realise he was hungry. And what about coffee? Right now, he desperately needed a caffeine fix.

But before he could even take in the sight of the shop, his ears heard a song: *Beautiful In My Eyes*, by Joshua Kadison, played gently through the speakers. *And love songs! Of bloody course there'd be love songs. Gemma!*

And there she was: his next victim. The person he was going to rip apart and turn inside out, all for the sake of a quick buck. Well, the book wasn't quick, by any stretch of his imagination, but the bucks would be good, and the advance had been deliciously handsome, allowing him to invest in a ranch down south.

When she lifted her head to the sound of the doorbells, Soraya smiled at the handsome tourist and said 'Welcome to the House of Hearts. If there's anything I can do to help you, please ask. All of our pieces are one of a kind. Here,' she said, proffering a basket as he walked up to the counter. 'Help yourself to a cookie.'

Simon Beaudin was lost for words. Had he just stepped into an alternative reality? The most gorgeous woman he'd ever seen in his life made hand-crafted hearts and offering him fresh-from-the-oven gingerbread cookies.

'They're home made,' she said, when he didn't reach forward. In all these years, no one had *ever* refused her cookies or hesitated. 'They're gluten-free, dairy-free, egg-free.'

Simon allowed himself to smile. 'Is there anything left in them then?' he asked, laughing; and reaching for one, he was struck by how beautiful her eyes were. Their hands brushed, and they both stepped back such was the spark as skin touched skin. As they tried to avoid each other's gaze, Simon found it was impossible to look away. It was as if each of them had magnets inserted into their rapidly dilating pupils. Despite never having met before, there was a sense of familiarity that he found unsettling. Something that went way beyond words or memories. It was a feeling so comfortable that he felt somewhat uncomfortable trying to make sense of it all.

'Thank you,' he said, taking a bite. 'Mmm. What's in them? I know what *isn't* in here, but…what is that taste? I can't quite place it.'

Without answering, she asked 'Where have you travelled from? You're not from around here, are you?'

'New York. Is there anywhere that I can buy a coffee in town? I couldn't see anywhere.'

'I'll make you a coffee!' she smiled, and said 'Don't go away. Make yourself at home. I'll be right back!'

And just like that, she was gone, up the spiral staircase at the rear of shop, humming all the way, her long, floating pink skirt swishing around her legs. Simon did a double take: She wasn't wearing shoes, just thick woolly pink socks. Was he seriously going to consider her as a successful business owner? The woman wasn't even dressed properly!

As Simon's thoughts raced, he tried to ignore the physical sensations coming to life in his body. *What the hell just happened?*, he asked himself. There wasn't a time in his life where his skin reacted to a woman's touch the way that it just had. He lifted his briefcase up onto the counter to grab his Dictaphone. He was going to record everything. Not for one second did he trust himself to think straight if she was going to be in the same room.

Simon wandered around the shop. There were hearts from wall to wall, from floor to ceiling, from table to table. And yet, despite it being a shrine to love, it didn't feel crowded or suffocating. Everything was tasteful. Not a gaudy heart in sight. He noticed that, like she'd said, no two hearts were the same. At the long window seat, he stood looking down the stretch of the main street. What an unusual place. *No coffee shop!*

Simon sat at the window seat, heart-shaped cushions behind his back, and deep-red fairy lights twinkling in the window. It was a little girl's idea of heaven, but as a grown man—a prominent and respected voice in the finance industry—he felt distinctly out of place there in his suit.

The woodstove on the other side of the room was crackling, keeping the whole shop cosy warm. The wooden floors were polished with beeswax, and a subtle honey scent wafted through the room as if in a tango with the competing spices from the cookies.

Simon spoke into the recording device: *Everything is handmade, and one of a kind, yet the price tickets on them don't indicate that they're overly expensive; not that I know what a love heart should cost!*

Just then, the door opened and a young man walked in with the post. He smiled at Simon, said 'Good morning', and dropped the mail on the counter, then filled his pocket with cookies. 'Best cookies ever!' The postman laughed as he walked out the door.

'Here's your coffee, sir,' Soraya smiled as she placed a tray with the cafetiere and cups beside him on the window seat. 'Sure is a picture-perfect day, isn't it?'

Was this woman for real? Gorgeous, attentive, kind, happy. Perhaps a bit too Pollyanna-ish for his taste, but beautiful and friendly nevertheless. One thing was for sure: he'd never met a woman like her in his whole life.

'Sugar, cream, honey, milk?' she asked, failing to declare it was decaff.

'Black is perfect,' he said. 'Thank you.'

When she made him a sweet creamy coffee, and sprinkled cinnamon and nutmeg on top, he looked on in disbelief. Didn't she hear him say *black*?

'No, you don't want black coffee, sir,' she said, as if reading his mind. 'You'll never want black coffee again after you've had mine.'

*Gemma, you're going to pay for this!* Simon felt increasingly furious that he'd driven all this way. For what? A fruitcake of a woman who wouldn't even let him have his coffee the way he liked? Just give me the damn coffee black, he wanted to say, but he realised he had trouble even being angry at her. Hell, even her elbow was gorgeous!

Reluctantly, he took a sip, and surprised himself at just how good it tasted. He took another, and was immediately thinking of having a second cup. She's right, he admitted to himself. It did taste great. How was that even possible?

Simon looked her up and down. Everything about her feminine curves had him forgetting the sole purpose of his visit to House of Hearts. His mind was elsewhere.

Soraya looked up at him and smiled, making herself comfortable beside him on the window seat.

'How does this town run without coffee?' he asked, taking another sip. When her face dipped, as if a cloud passed over the Sun causing a shadow to descend across the whole town, she stood up, aborting the flow of coffee into her cup.

'What's wrong?' he asked.

'I've just made you coffee. Isn't this real enough for you?'

'I didn't mean that. This is lovely, I just meant... there's no coffee shop.'

Soraya turned and walked back to her work space. Clearly he'd upset her, which hadn't been his intention. Simon poured the rest of the coffee into her cup, added cream and honey and then sprinkled her spice mixture on top. Somewhat chastened, he moved determinedly towards her.

'I'm so sorry. I didn't intend to upset you. I simply meant...'

'No harm caused,' she said, avoiding eye contact. Soraya picked up her ledger and began to input figures. 'Let me know if there's anything I can help you with.'

He *had* upset her!

Simon drank the rest of his coffee, and just as he swilled the last mouthful, the bells at the door rang out their message of love: a customer.

A well-dressed businessman came bounding into the shop, casting half an eye at Simon, then walked up to Soraya.

'Good morning,' he said. 'Soraya, you're crying. Whatever is the matter?' he asked, as he reached over to touch her hand. This wasn't the Soraya the township knew and loved. This wasn't the happy-go-lucky, positive-every-single-day woman who kept this town alive with her sheer joy and vivaciousness for every extraordinary day. Not at all.

Simon stood up, horrified. Had he made her cry? All at once, he joined the businessman at the counter. He had to fix this, and fast. If he didn't, there was no way she'd let him interview her.

'I'm fine, Dennis. Dust in my eye. Cookies are straight from the oven,' she said, plastering a smile across her face, and then turned her back.

The man was about to leave when he caught Simon's eye.

'Hello,' he said, 'funny, you look exactly like Simon Beaudin, that famous financial TV journalist. Of course, you'd never find a man like that in a business like this,' he chuckled.

Simon held out his hand to shake. 'Hi. I'm Simon Beaudin.'

The man stumbled over his own name: 'I'm Dennis Dyson, bank manager of Rainbow Valley. I read all of your articles and watch your morning report. You're on sabbatical, right now, aren't you? What are you doing here? On holidays with your family?'

Simon noticed that Soraya had turned around and was looking him firmly in the eye. It was clear that he had some explaining to do, pronto!

'I'm here on business, actually. Good to meet you Dennis.'

Dennis left the shop, looking behind him in awe.

'The Coffee House is down a narrow alley behind the Post Office,' Soraya said matter of factly. You'll get black coffee there. Opens from 11am till 3pm, six days a week.'

'Your coffee was perfect,' he said, meaning every word, and realised he should probably get straight to the point. 'I've come here to ask if you'd allow me to interview you for a book I'm writing on recession-proof businesses. My colleague, Gemma West, recommended House of Hearts. I'm still not entirely sure if she was serious or sending me on a goose chase because I haven't asked her out on a date,' he smiled, and noticed that Soraya almost fell for the look on his face. *Almost.*

Soraya studied him for a full thirty seconds before speaking. 'Gemma? Gemma who works as a PA for some flash financial publication? Shaved head, too many earrings for one ear, but amazing dress sense?'

'I don't know about her dress sense, but as for the hair and earrings, yes, that's her.'

'Oh no,' Soraya said, her hand falling over her heart. 'You're all wrong for her. She needs someone who...' And then she stopped. 'I'm sorry, you don't need to know who the right person for her is and I'm just talking too much. Cookie?' She handed him the basket. Simon surprised himself by following local tradition and taking a handful rather than just one.

A customer came in before they could resume their conversation.

Simon made himself comfortable back at the window seat, and noted how the woman was deeply enchanted by the shop. But, for the most part, he simply couldn't take his eyes of Soraya Juniper.

The customer was in her thirties, and immediately grabbed five bespoke hearts and took them to the counter.

'My cousin insisted I come to this place. Magic, she called it. And right she was,' she said in a thick cockney accent. 'I'm in town for a few days. I'm sure I'll be back again.'

Soraya smiled, and then wrapped up the hearts. One was woven willow. 'Hang this over your bed to bring you harmony in your dreams,' she said. And when she wrapped up the apron with ruby hearts embroidered along the edge, she whispered 'Always prepare food with love.' When it came to the three lavender bags, she simply popped them into packaging. 'Just wait a moment, will you?' Soraya asked her customer.

Simon's eyes followed her as she made her way across the room. Soraya's every movement was graceful and ethereal, like that of a young doe darting through woodland. Fragile, yet confident; beautiful and vulnerable. How was it even possible that he found himself wanting to protect her? She was a complete stranger!

'This one is a gift from me,' Soraya said holding up the stained-glass heart, and allowed the daylight to shine through it. 'This will break so easily if you don't look after it with care. Do the same with your heart. Don't give it to someone who'll be careless with your feelings.' And for a second, Simon was sure she quickly looked over at him as she said those words. *Was she talking about him?*

The customer left, as if walking on air, giggling as she headed out into the main street.

'You just gave away one of your products. How do you make money if you give cookies and hearts away?'

'She needed that heart.' Soraya looked deeply into his eyes.

Simon felt as if she was reaching into and reading the deepest parts of his soul. It unnerved him. Damn it, he was here to interview her, not to be 'read' like he was an open book. When she didn't say anything else and kept looking at him, he found himself stumbling for words to retrieve some normality.

'So, may I interview you? I'm assuming that given you're still in business, your business is, indeed, recession proof?'

'My business is more than viable, Mr Beaudin, but I don't see that the business world I live in would be of relevance to your target readership. No. No, I don't want to be interviewed,' she said firmly but kindly, and reached into a sewing kit to begin making a new heart. 'Thank you for asking, though.'

It was the coffee! The damn coffee. If only he'd been grateful and shut his mouth, then he'd have scored an interview. Still, he was a master at getting people to change their minds and open up. This woman was no different to anyone else when it came down to it. Though, he did have his work cut out for him. Simon would probably have to spend a few more hours in this town than he expected to, and his mind raced as he mentally prepared his arsenal for a charm offensive. Whatever he had to do to get her to cooperate, he'd do it. After all, that was his job.

Soraya looked up, surprised to find him still sitting there. 'Is there anything else I can help you with?'

Simon had to admit: she was beautiful. There was no question about it. Odd, maybe; fancy telling people what sort of heart they needed! Quirky and beautiful. Easily distracted, he found himself drawn in by her long layered locks of chocolate-brown hair, which hung in gentle waves around her shoulders. Her skin had a healthy olive glow, almost as if she were of Mediterranean origin. Simon noticed that she didn't wear makeup, but then she didn't need to. Her lashes were long and hung down rather lazily; and her cheeks had a natural flush to them. Simon was utterly sidetracked by her ring finger. Empty. Bare. Vacant. Naked. He stopped that train of thought right there. Had men been scared off by her heart obsession? Simon couldn't imagine that a woman so beautiful would be left on the shelf for so long. It seemed incongruous. Sure, she might be light years away from the kind of women he was used to working with and dating, but she was lovely. Loveable. As the words began floating around his head, he could have kicked himself. What was in that damn coffee? Why couldn't he think straight? Normally coffee wired him up, instantly, and he'd be firing on all cylinders for a fourteen-hour day, but now, he just wanted to curl up on a comfortable sofa: with *her*.

'Is there a Mr Juniper?' Did he actually just ask that? Did he say it out loud? And then, he knew, by the look on her face, that he did, indeed, speak those words. The same dark shadow that fell over her face earlier, returned; she frowned, then turned away.

'My father, Mr Juniper, lives several hours from here.'

'I wasn't meaning your father.'

'I know.'

'Is there a man in your life?' he continued prodding. Clearly he'd hit a tender spot.

'No, Mr Beaudin, there is not a man in my life. Now, if there isn't anything I can do for you, I need to get on with my work.'

And just like that, she cut him off. The attraction wasn't one-sided, he knew that, so why was she fobbing him off so badly?

'Do you mind if I stay a little longer before I make the long drive home?'

Could she be guilt-driven into an interview, he wondered.

'Yes, you may, but you might prefer Mabel's Coffee House.'

'I doubt it's as lovely as House of Hearts.'

Did she just raise her eyebrows? So, she has a sarcastic side. Not all Pollyanna and sunshine then? Simon was starting to wonder just how many personalities she had.

'Flattery only works when it's sincere, Mr Beaudin. I won't be flattered into an interview, nor into bed.'

He was about to tell her to call him Simon, and that Mr Beaudin was way too formal, but then he heard the word *bed*. Surely the virginal-looking Soraya wasn't suggesting that he might be interested in her?

Where on Earth was he going to take the conversation from here? He quickly realised that she was one perceptive woman and there was no way he was going to be able to take advantage of her in any sense of the word. How had she managed to spin this around on him? For God's sake, Simon thought, I'm the one used to dissecting people, and seeing through them; and she's doing the very same thing to me. No one had ever played him at his own game before. Frankly, he was a little speechless.

'Bed? Now there's an idea. I wasn't trying to flatter you for either thing. I genuinely like the feeling in this place. The ambience, as Gemma calls it. I hold my hand up and say that I was sceptical, and that I thought Gemma was pulling my leg...'

'But you drove four hours to get here...why would you do that if you thought it was a joke? You must have believed. You must have known deep inside that this wasn't a joke.'

'You got me there. It was a long way to drive. I'd have phoned, but Gemma said the shop doesn't have a phone. Not to mention you don't have a website!'

'That's right. I like my privacy and I like peace,' she said, unapologetically.

The heart bells rang out.

'Good morning, welcome to the House of Hearts,' Soraya beamed at the couple who entered. 'Do let me know if there's anything I can help you with.'

Simon found himself thinking about that bed she'd mentioned, and about what it would be like to wake up to that smile every morning. Gemma! He recalled her words: *it might just change your life.*

Simon wondered what gift Soraya would give to this couple. They were hand in hand, probably married a few dozen years, and gleefully headed to the counter. Before they'd even arrived at the counter, Soraya extended the cookie basket. 'Would you like a gingerbread heart? They've not long been out of the oven. Don't worry, they're soft,' she promised, reading their thoughts about false teeth and cookies.

Simon wondered if she could actually read minds. Or was it just years of experience that had her so well-tuned to customers?

The man and his wife were in the shop for over an hour, and Simon kept looking at his watch. Still no closer to an interview, and no sign of the lovebirds leaving anytime soon. Maybe he should go to the coffee shop and grab an espresso.

Where was Soraya? When did she leave the room? Where did she go? Why wasn't he paying attention to her instead of texting Gemma?

And then a couple of minutes later, the softest of sounds came from the spiral staircase as Soraya entered the shop with a cafetiere. 'More coffee?' she smiled.

Did he have caffeine withdrawal written all over his face? How did she know? Was Soraya Juniper psychic?

'That would be lovely. Thank you, Soraya. Will you join me?'

Before she had a chance to answer, the elderly gentleman was at the counter ready to pay for his purchases.

'Did you find everything you were looking for?' she asked him.

'I did indeed. I have a question, though. May I play your piano?'

'Yes please! I'm always hoping that people will play when they're in here. The locals do, but tourists aren't usually so keen. Go head, there are books inside the piano stool if you need them.'

Simon thought she looked like she was going to clap her hands with glee. How was it that she could go from grown business woman to excited little girl in a nanosecond, and then back again? Soraya perched herself on the window seat, and began to hum to the tune he was playing: *We've Only Just Begun*, by The Carpenters.

'Oh, that is so romantic,' she whispered. 'They're so in love!'

'The way you're smiling, it seems like their joy means as much to you as it does to them.'

'It does!' She finished humming the song, and then let out a loud applause. 'How long have you been together?' she asked breathlessly, walking over to the piano. If Simon didn't know any better, he would have thought she'd skipped there. He rubbed his eyes as if to bring himself back to reality, but everything before him was still the same. Was Soraya Juniper real or just a figment of his imagination?

'Seventy years today. And never a cross word between us,' the lady said, reaching for her husband's hand.

Tears sprung to Soraya's eyes. 'That's simply beautiful. Let me play you a piece so you may dance together. I couldn't bear the thought of you leaving this shop without dancing upon these floorboards.'

The couple embraced, and Simon watched in disbelief. When she played, much to Simon's complete surprise, Soraya began to sing: *When You Say Nothing At All*.

There really must have been something in the coffee, because, to his utter amazement, Simon was soon standing by the old piano and joining in the chorus.

For a hard-nosed financial journalist, Soraya was astonished by his tone. Sure, he had a mellifluous speaking voice that clearly commanded respect, but his singing voice was melodic, sweet, and somehow masculine and virile, suggesting aspects of his personality which hadn't occurred to her before. It was deeply resonant, and she almost felt it vibrating throughout her being. There were parts of her body that were flipping in somersaults, and being awoken: places that had lain dormant for years and years. Places, she thought, which would never, *could never*, come to life again.

Maybe Simon Beaudin wasn't too bad after all. Then she mentally chastised herself. It was a silly thought. A man like him would never look twice at a woman like her.

The couple introduced themselves as Alice and Murray, and said that it was the best present they could ever have had.

'I've not finished yet,' Soraya said. 'If you think you can manage those spiral steps, you can have a complimentary night on me, staying in my B&B upstairs. The evening comes with a massage by Shona—she's brilliant; a three-course meal in the restaurant upstairs, with a string quartet for company; a leisurely soak in the outdoor hot tub—towels and robes included—and breakfast in bed. What do you say? Please say yes!'

Alice and Murray turned to each other. 'Oh my! Really? That would be wonderful. Yes, yes please! Book us in.' Alice laughed out loud, and Murray squeezed her tightly.

'Fabulous. Let me call Shona and the quartet. The room is free for the next few days, so anytime is fine by me.'

Soraya almost danced a little jig of triumph after she finished her second call.

'Tonight it is then! Come by anytime from five, and I'll show you your room.'

They left the shop in a dream, as love sick as the day they first met.


'You just gave them what is probably worth hundreds of dollars. How do you make money when you give so much away?'

'Not everything is about money, Mr Beaudin!'

'Simon.'

'Simon,' she repeated, as if to etch his name firmly into her vocabulary of important words. 'There are some things in this world that money can't buy. Obviously there is a value to what I'll be giving them tonight, but they've given me something today. Something that's priceless. They've given me hope, and faith, and an affirmation that everything I do here is about one thing: love.'

'If you believe in love, then why isn't there a man in your life? Or, is there a woman?'

'I love my customers, Mr... *Simon*.'

'Is that enough?'

'What sort of question is that? Do I look like I'm deficient in something? Do I seem unhappy? My life is complete. I don't need anyone.'

'Not needing anyone isn't the same as choosing someone, or being chosen.'

'No, I suspect it's not.' And then, changing the subject, she asked: 'Fancy a bite of lunch?'

'You are going to let me start paying for my food and drinks, aren't you?'

'No. No I'm not,' she said, as if he'd asked the world's silliest question. How did she have the capacity to make him feel like a foolish schoolboy? What happened to the man? The man who was drawn to her as if she were the air he needed to survive.

'Watch the shop for me, will you?' she asked without waiting for a reply, then skipped up the staircase.

Although she'd only been gone for ten minutes, within that time eight people came in and made purchases. Simon was grateful that they'd all paid cash, because he had no idea how to use the old-fashioned card machine. Simon felt as if he was supposed to give them a free heart, but instead he offered cookies.

As the last customer left the shop, Soraya emerged with a tray of food. Upon an oak chopping board, was a selection of savoury temptations: olives, feta cheese, ciabatta, sundried tomatoes, basil leaves, and marinated artichokes.

'Why are you looking after me in such style, when I unintentionally offended you earlier?'

'You look like you need feeding, that's all. Now eat up.'

Miraculously, or at least to his mind, not a single customer came in while they ate. She asked him nonstop questions about his work, his life, his past. If he didn't know better, he'd think she was interviewing him. The woman didn't leave a stone unturned. Somehow she even excavated longlost loves and brief affairs, though he did he best to lightly skim over that particular topic.

'So you like women, then?' she asked thoughtfully.

'Did I give you the idea that I don't?'

'No, just wondering why you have such an aversion to love.'

'Strange as it might be for you to believe, I was very moved by Alice and Murray, and I'd wish that for every couple who walks down the aisle. My experience, however, is that I don't have anyone in my personal circle who has a love like that.'

'That doesn't mean you have to avoid love, does it?'

And there she was again, flipping everything back to him. Always asking him questions...poking, prodding, establishing, and dissecting.

'Do you want to be in love?' she asked, clearing up their lunch plates.

'I've not thought about it, Soraya. My life is full, with work. I'm always in meetings, travelling about.'

'I didn't ask if your life was full, Simon. I asked if you wanted to be in love.'

This time he was not going to give her the satisfaction of an answer.

'Let me help you tidy these up,' he said, and then 'Show me the way.'

Soraya faltered for a moment.

Was he going to follow her upstairs? To her home? To her sanctuary?

'It's fine. I can manage,' she insisted.

'You have left me in no doubt that you're capable of doing anything you set your mind to, but I want to help.' Simon watched her every step as she walked to the front door, and put up the Back-in-Five-Minutes sign, then headed up the stairs. He was close behind, breathing in the scent of rose petals which seemed to follow her everywhere. It was a distinctly different scent to that cloying perfume-rich world of the newspaper office. He liked it. He liked her. He could even grow to love her. In a different lifetime, perhaps. Not this one. Their worlds were too different. *They* were too different.

# Behind Closed Doors

'This is the dining area,' Soraya said, leading Simon into a simply decorated restaurant. There was only one table, and it was already set with a white linen cloth, candelabra, and red roses. The floorboards were polished with beeswax, and the loosely hung curtains were white georgette. As the fabric moved gently against the breeze, Simon found himself drawn to the French doors leading to the balcony.

'You've created a beautiful space in here. It's intimate.' He didn't say anything else for a few moments, but Soraya found herself looking at him and wondering what a hard-nosed financial journalist could possibly know about intimacy.

'It's almost as if you set the stage so completely for lovers that they have no choice but to be on their best behaviour,' he laughed.

Was that a compliment or an insult, she wondered. 'Some people need the stage before they can trust their feelings,' she replied, feeling a little defensive.

'Soraya, it was a compliment.'

'Oh.'


Simon wandered around the room, taking in the subtle scents: beeswax, rose oil, fresh air. Combined with the Shaker-style simplicity, it blended to create an ambience of peace, romance and stillness: a template for going within to one's feelings, and not being distracted by external prompts.

'I bring in a quartet to play while the lovers dine, and they can dance afterwards if they like.'

'There is no question that House of Hearts is

unique. I can't say I've ever been in a restaurant that only seats two people.'

'Oh, Simon, don't be fooled by the two chairs! The two chairs make a statement.'

For a moment, he wanted to laugh at the shocked expression on her face. There was something intriguing about her: she could go from mature business woman, to innocent girl, to carefree teenager, to mindful human in the space of seconds. Simon wanted to capture her essence, not for his book, but for the rest of his life. Don't be crazy! He chided himself. Chalk and cheese have never been a winning combination!

'There are never just two people in a relationship. Whether we like it or not, we bring every relationship we've ever had with us to the table.'

'Well, when you look at it that way…' he offered a little too sheepishly for comfort.

'That's the only way to look at it. And besides, our previous relationships shape us. They help us to grow and to become a better person.'

'Not always! Some relationships are poisonous.'

'That's true, but we learn from that. We move on.'

'Have you been in a poisonous relationship, Soraya?' He wasn't entirely sure where those words came from, but it was too late to retract them now.

'No. I haven't,' she said, then turned away and fiddled with some items on the oak dresser. Simon wasn't letting her end this conversation so easily.

'So, at the risk of asking the obvious, why are you single now? If the relationships were so happy and healthy…' He stopped, then, in midsentence when she looked up at him with a frown on her face. It was as if he'd punched her in the stomach; her whole face reflected nothing but pain.

'Mr Beaudin,' she said, returning to a more formal footing. 'Some relationships aren't meant to last forever.'

Simon followed her as she left the room and indicated the next room they were going into.

'This is the restaurant kitchen. Aren't the views over the mountains just breathtaking?'

How does she keep doing that? he wondered. How does she keep changing the conversation as if it never even happened?

'Would you like to help me prepare their meal tonight? It would give you some more insight into House of Hearts.'

'Why not?' he laughed. 'My cooking skills might fall a bit short, though.'

'I'm sure I can put you to good use,' she smiled, and for a second, just a second, he wondered if she was flirting with him. There was a spark in her eyes as she smiled; a spark so bright it could have lit New York City.

'This is the honeymoon suite,' she said, but words weren't necessary.

'Love nest would be a better description,' he chuckled. 'It's enough to make me want to…' he caught her face flush crimson, and discontinued his train of thought.

'The views are amazing. Is that the same river I drove over when I came into Rainbow Valley?'

'Yes, it's gorgeous, isn't it? And over there, that meadow leads you to a shortcut up Amber Mountain.

'Have you grown up here, in this area?' he asked, hoping he wasn't treading on challenging ground again.

'More or less, yes.' She opened the window a little wider to let some more fresh air in, and then prepared the woodstove with kindling and small logs. 'My grandparents live here, and I spent every school holiday with them. I fell in love with the place. My parents lived here for a while, but moved away a few years ago.'

'What work do you need to do before Alice and Murray arrive later?'

'Just the meal. The bed has fresh linen. The hot tub is heating. The quartet is arranged.

'Soraya, I know I was skeptical about this place, but please let me say this: I am impressed with your venture. It defies logic in terms of money making, but for some reason you manage to make it work. You survive without the Internet or even a phone for goodness sake, and yet you're never without customers.'

'It's called word of mouth, Simon. Never underestimate the power of storytelling.' She smiled, and said 'We're done up here.'

'What about your home? Where do you live? Aren't there more rooms up here? Another floor? I'm sure I saw...'

'Yes, I live up here, but you don't need to see that.'

'I'd like to though,' he smiled at her, not intending to make her melt like butter, but he quickly became aware that she was not immune to his smile or charm. At the increasing change to her skin colour, he asked 'May I?'

She raised her eyebrows as if she were a teenager being forced against her will.

Soraya led Simon up another flight of stairs. 'This is my home,' she said quietly as they entered her lounge.

'Not a heart in sight,' he whispered. 'I don't understand.'

Simon tried to read her face, searching for clues. It didn't make sense. The woman was obsessed with hearts, and yet, as far as he could see, there wasn't a single one in her home.

'I guess not,' she said lightly, trying to downplay the stark contrast. 'Customers don't come up here, so they're not necessary.'

'Maybe not for them, but what about for you?'

'Me?'

He could tell that she wasn't sure how to answer the question, and instead led him to the kitchen. Simon didn't follow her all the way, though. He stared back into the lounge and was taken in by her exquisite decorating skills. 'Did you work in interior design before you opened House of Hearts? You have an incredible touch with colour and style.'

'No. I just like things to be beautiful, that's all.'

'Everything about this place is beautiful. You've woven yourself into every room. You are simply everywhere. It's enchanting.'

'Mr Beaudin, are you saying I'm beautiful?'

'I am indeed.' And that's where they stood for the next few moments, just a few feet apart, looking into each other's eyes. Neither of them could find words, but in truth, they weren't looking for them. They were reading each other, sinking into the depths of the person in front of them. Simon was the first to move. He knew that if he didn't, he'd have no choice: he'd have to kiss her.

'So, is this a kitchen through here?' he asked, catching his breath and adjusting his tie. His tie! It seemed so ridiculously formal. What had he been thinking? No wonder he hadn't made progress in securing an interview. He should have approached her on a more friendly level.

'Yes. It's small, but there's only me to cook for.'

Although she said the words lightly, they cut deep into his heart. How was it possible for someone so beautiful, so kind, so generous, to be so...so *alone*.

Simon took off his jacket and tie, and placed them over the back of a dining chair. 'Soraya, can we start again? I approached you the wrong way. I came here with my business head on and barged in without any consideration for the fact you are nothing like the business people I normally deal with.'

'Okay,' she said softly.

He held out his hand. 'Hi. I'm Simon. I'm a writer, and I wonder if I could interview you about House of Hearts. And' he felt himself fumble for the words he so desperately wanted to say '...and about the woman behind House of Hearts.'

'You lost me at the woman behind House of Hearts. I don't actually want to share my personal life with anyone.'

Simon's heart sank. Back to square one. Why was she such hard work?

'Fine. Just the business, then?'

Soraya frowned again. For a woman who kept so much of herself private, her face was transparent.

Simon thought he'd try one of her tactics, and changed the subject.

'And there are more rooms, aren't there?'

Flustered, she answered, 'Just my bedroom and the attic room.'

'May I?'

'See my bedroom? Why?'

'Why not?' he smiled, melting her frosty guard before she erected too many ice bricks.

'Because...'

'It's private?' he laughed. 'I'm not asking you to

go to bed with me, just asking to look at the room. I'm curious as to how you decorated it, that's all.'

'Just to be clear, Simon, I'm not sleeping with you.'

And he followed that scent of rose petals up the final flight of stairs.

Soraya didn't enter her room, but opened the door and gestured for him to go inside. 'Another beautiful room. You are the queen of minimalism, aren't you?'

'There's a lot to be said for simplicity. Clutter isn't healthy.'

Simon surveyed the décor. The bedhead was carved from oak, and matched a set of drawers and a slim wardrobe. The linen, cushions and curtains were sage green, counter-balanced with white. Not an item was out of place, and yet it looked loved and lived in as if she'd spent most of her time in here. He wondered about her, and what she did when she was alone in this room. Did she read? Did she daydream? And then he felt a pang beneath his firm pectoral muscles. Perhaps she cried in here? He wasn't entirely sure where such a thought came from, but it threw him off kilter.

She was standing by the window watching the world outside as people moved from shop to shop along the main street of Rainbow Valley.

'Sure is busy out there this afternoon,' she said, as if deliberately wanting to interrupt his thoughts. 'Shall we head back downstairs now?'

'There's another room, though.'

'Oh, that's just an attic. Nothing to see up there.'

Simon probably wouldn't have thought much of it except for the fact that she studiously avoided eye contact as she said it.

What was she hiding this time?

'I'd love to see it. The view must be even better than this one. May I?'

And it was that transparent face of hers that clinched it for him. There was something up there!

'Really Simon, the view is just as good from here.'

'Can I be the judge of that?'

When they stepped onto the landing, Soraya reached up with a hook and pulled down a thick rope, and then pulled down the door to the attic.

'Let me get that,' Simon offered, and then released the folded-up wooden stepladder that was attached to it.

'I'll wait here,' she said nervously. 'It's too small for two people.'

'Okay.'

Simon climbed the ladder, expecting to see a cramped space filled with storage boxes. What he found was a compact room containing a double bed, a writing desk, laptop, phone and printer. There was barely room to move.

'The modern world does exist here at the House of Hearts. Phone, internet, laptop. And here I was thinking you were a Luddite. You had me fooled, Soraya.' His laughter stopped abruptly, though, when he saw a framed photo of Soraya with a handsome man. They were smiling and looking lovingly into each other's eyes. The scenery was familiar. It was the bridge at the entry to Rainbow Valley. Simon studied her face. In the photo, she looked like a different woman: light and happy.

'Have you seen enough?' Soraya called up the ladder.

'Just admiring the beautiful view,' he replied, taking in every inch of her gorgeous face. It was wonderful to be able to look at her without causing her to blush, and to indulge himself in how she made him feel.

'I need to get back to the shop, Simon.'

'I'll join you in a minute,' he answered.

'I'll see you there, then.'

Simon stayed in the attic for at least twenty minutes, admiring her face and trying to read her eyes. For years, he'd read people's body language to get to the core of who they were, but there was something about Soraya that, despite her transparency about so many things, he simply couldn't read. She was an enigma to him.

When he entered the shop, he could see that she was visibly relieved. There were some customers cluttered by the bookshelves, chatting away happily with each other. Simon made himself comfortable at the window seat, and noticed that she'd made him another cup of coffee. But he nearly choked on it when the customers paid for their items and the total came to more than four hundred dollars.

'Not bad for a few minutes of work,' he said politely after the customers left the shop.

'The labour in those items is worth far more than you can see. Those books were written by people who spent months, maybe even years, writing. They might look like cheap paperbacks to you, but they involved a lot of work.'

'Soraya, let me ask you this: if I came in as a customer, what heart would you give me?'

She laughed. 'You don't really want me to answer that, do you?'

'What's so funny?'

'Never mind.' She pottered around at the counter, tidying up pens, paper, and craft supplies. 'I'll be shutting the shop in ten minutes, and then I need to prepare tonight's meal for Alice and Murray.'

Soraya looked Simon up and down, as if studying him in great detail. Now it was his turn to flush scarlet.

'Simon, I've decided that you can interview me for your book, but it's only on one condition.'

What made her change her mind? Simon was desperate to ask her, but thought better of it.

'Sure, anything. What is it?'

'You need to stay here, at House of Hearts, for at least a week. Anything less than that and you won't be able to write about this business accurately. You need to get a sense of what I do here, and about this town.'

'So you're an all-or-nothing woman, then?' In that moment, they both sensed themselves tumbling to a place that was wholly new and unfamiliar. Soraya felt herself smiling without any guards in place. Was she finally starting to trust him? Simon loved how open she was when she smiled: eyes lit up, shoulders relaxed, dimples alive. Beautiful.

# The Dance of Love

The afternoon continued at a gentle pace, with Simon delegated to chopping onions and crushing garlic. 'These aren't exactly the foods of lovers, you know?' He said, as tears fell from his eyes while chopping the second onion.

'After seventy years of marriage, I think they can both handle a bit of garlic!'

'What do you think is the key to a long and happy marriage like Alice and Murray have?' he asked.

'Respect. Far too many people treat their partner shabbily after the honeymoon phase is over. If the awe they had at the beginning of the relationship was cultivated on a daily basis, their love would thrive.'

'What happened after your honeymoon phase?' He asked her tenderly, but even so, her pain was evident and fell like a shadow across her face. Simon's mind raced at the possibilities. Had she been treated badly? But if so, then why have the guy's photo in a frame?

'I never made it to the honeymoon phase.' And when she looked into Simon's eyes, he sensed that she'd shared something deep and precious and was entrusting him not to damage a treasure.

'I'm sorry.' He put down his chopping knife, and washed his hands. 'May I ask what happened?'

'We're making a meal for lovers here; I really don't want to feed them my love story by infusing their food with pain. Let's just keep the conversation on an even keel.'

And there was that roadblock again, so carefully crafted and engineered to keep the traffic moving in a different direction.

'Maybe later? Tonight, perhaps?'

'Maybe. Here, can you chop these?'

Well, that was the end of that. Non-committal, and subject over.

'What exactly are we preparing here?' Simon asked.

'I always try and use local and seasonal foods. It gives the meal an authenticity that you wouldn't otherwise have. It helps the couple to feel closer to the Earth. Not that they'd know that, but it does. Tonight's meal is artichokes braised in lemon and olive oil, followed by a spicy green salad with pears. The main dish is wild-mushroom pie served with kale, garlic and cranberries. I collect the mushrooms from the woods, not far from here. It's a simple dish, but ever so more-ish. It's impossible to have one serving.'

Simon watched her unfold like a fern in springtime as she prepared the ingredients into the assorted dishes. It fascinated him how alive she was in the kitchen, as if the vegetables were friends she'd had over for an afternoon chat. More than once he found himself drowning in her smiling eyes and laughter.

'What's the pumpkin for?' he asked, as she took a baby roast butternut from the oven.

'This is for dessert.'

'Sweet pumpkin pie?' he asked.

'Roasted-pumpkin ice cream with miso, butterscotch and black sesame crumble. I'll save you some. It's divine.'

'I have no doubt about that,' he said. 'I had no idea you were a gourmet cook. Why didn't you open a restaurant?'

'I *do* have a restaurant,' she said, shaking her head. 'Do you think it's less meaningful because I have two customers rather than 20 or 200?'

Simon placed his hands on her shoulders, and steadied her in front of him. 'I always seem to say the wrong thing to you. It's not my intention. I was complimenting you on your cooking skills, and somehow it's come out the wrong way.'

'Oh, I understood you perfectly, Simon. You know, maybe by the time you leave here you'll come to understand that not everything in life is about money.'

'Touché!'

He didn't say anything else, but held her gaze.

'What?' she asked. 'Don't tell me you want to 'start again'? You can't keep going back to the beginning of our relationship every time we disagree on something.'

'You're rather feisty when you get going, aren't you?' he laughed. 'Do you know what I'd like to do right now?'

'Check up on the stock exchange?' she muttered, raising her eyebrows.

'No, I'd like to kiss you.'

'Oh.'

When her eyes cast downwards, Simon wondered if she was actually contemplating the possibility. 'I don't think that's a good idea,' she said. 'Wouldn't it be a conflict of interest? I mean, how could you write a non-biased piece on this place if you did that?'

She was talking quickly now, far too quickly. Was she talking herself out of something that she actually desired? Simon wondered if she was nervous.

'As I recall, I'm not allowed to write about the woman behind the shop, just about the business. No conflict of interest at all. Is that a yes, then?'

'You haven't asked me anything?'

Simon loosened his grip on her shoulders and he gently cupped the back of her head; and as he undid the loosely tied bun he watched as her hair fell down. Simon could see she was uneasy, not because she didn't want to be there, with him, but because she didn't know where they were heading. Already he got the sense that the future was not a place she ever dared think about. If he'd learned anything in their short time together, it was that the only moment she ever felt secure in was the present one. Over that, she had complete control.

Simon's arousal was determined to make its presence known, and as he leaned in towards her, they both felt a palpable sense of relief. This was where they wanted to be: in each other's arms. They held each other for several minutes, the bodily scents speaking to each other over the silence. It was as if they were home at long last. Simon could feel her heart rapidly beating against his chest. Now. Now was the perfect time to kiss her.

'May I kiss you, Soraya?'

It was a pointless question, as it was perfectly obvious that she'd say yes. Already, her body had leaned into his, too; he felt her beckoning him closer, so when she said 'No, we need to get this meal made,' Simon was left speechless.

'No?'

'There's no time. It's a little over an hour until they arrive, and I've got to get the ice-cream maker on, put the robes in their room in case they want to use the hot tub, and a few other jobs.'

'But surely you can spare a minute?'

'If you're going to kiss me Mr Beaudin, and I suspect by the end of this week that you probably will, then I want it to last for more than a minute!' She turned away quickly, so quickly, in fact, that he couldn't see the smile on her face.

'Have I upset you again? I seem to be making a habit of doing that!'

'No, you haven't upset me.' She tidied up the area around the kitchen sink, then excused herself to do a few little errands. 'Help yourself to coffee.'


Twenty minutes later, she returned to the kitchen to find Simon standing at the window watching the world of Rainbow Valley go about its business.

'Tell me more about your work,' Soraya asked, confident that she was on safe ground far away from kisses, hugs and bodily pleasures that felt too darned good for comfort. 'Why financial journalism?'

They chatted for some time, with Simon confiding that he'd never intended to end up in this line of work.

'What did you want to do?' Soraya asked, checking the ice cream for creaminess and solidity.

'Don't laugh, but I wanted to be a novelist. It was always my secret dream.'

'Why would I laugh at that?'

'Writing fiction isn't part of the real world.'

'Is that right?' she asked, raising her left eyebrow. 'Someone has to write those books. People don't tend to take non-fiction books with them when they go away on holiday. And besides, reading is a healthy pleasure.'

'My father didn't think it was a realistic choice. I was good at maths, so combined my skill with writing.'

'And do you love what you do?'

'Love what I do?'

'Yes, do you get out of bed each day excited by what you're contributing to the world? Do you feel this is your life's calling given that it's more realistic than writing stories?'

'Ever thought of being a guidance counsellor, Soraya?' he laughed, bringing his body to within inches of hers. 'I know, I know. There's no time to kiss.'

'How did you know what...'

'Because you're transparent!'

'Oh. *Oh*... Here, taste this,' she said, proffering a spoon with ice cream.

'Mmm. Mmmmm. That is so good!' He watched her smiling, and said, 'Were you trying to sidetrack me?'

'Did it work?'

'No!'

'The quartet will be here any minute to set up. Can you unlatch the back door of the shop so they can come in?' Soraya asked, diverting him from his lust-filled thoughts. 'I'm just going to double-check the guest bedroom and ensuite, then I'll show you out the back where the hot tub is and where I officiate wedding ceremonies.'

'No problem.' As he left the kitchen, Soraya's eyes never left his body. *Isn't it just amazing how your life can change*, she thought to herself. *Yesterday, I never knew anything was missing.*

Soraya headed up to the attic, switched the heating on, removed any sign of work-related business from the desk, and took the framed photo of her and Liam from the room. There were fresh sheets on the bed. Soraya fluffed up the pillows and tugged at the bedspread. She hoped he would be comfortable in this room, even though it was so tiny. Although she knew nothing about his home, she suspected he would be accustomed to spacious accommodation.

After putting the photo into her bedroom drawer, she headed downstairs and met Simon out the back.

'Do you like the hot tub?' she asked. 'Barnaby, the woodturner, built it for me. I just love how he's used local wood. I like the privacy too.'

'It's most definitely private. How often do you use it?'

'Me? I don't go in here. It's for guests.'

'You own it, Soraya, so why don't you treat yourself from time to time?'

'Too busy, I guess. Hey, come up here,' she said, changing the subject again. 'I'll take you up there while you're visiting. It's a beautiful walk through the woods. You'll love it. Even city boys like this walk,' she chuckled.

It was lovely to see her relax and laugh. Simon wanted to capture her essence and take it back to the city with him. An alien thought stabbed him in the centre of his chest. The city? It seemed so far away now. Like another lifetime. And the thought of being there again, doing his old job, living his old life, seemed incongruous. How was that even possible in less than a day? He dared to let his thoughts go a bit further: how would Soraya feel living in the city?

'What are you thinking about?' she asked as they strolled towards a gazebo and pond.

'I'm not entirely sure I can put it into words, Soraya. Yesterday, you were just a name. A business to study for my book. Today my life has been turned on its head and I don't know which way is up. You're making me see everything differently.'

'Don't worry, your life will be back to normal soon. You'll find your feet again.' She smiled it off, but as she turned away he saw the pain in her eyes.

'Soraya?'

And when she turned to look at him again, there was that smile, beaming as if she was the happiest person on the planet. The only thing was, he knew that wasn't true.

'This is where weddings are held. There aren't any bookings now until springtime. I love them, though. They're always small and intimate. We put up a marquee for the evening meal, and it's all catered for upstairs. My dad dug this pond by hand. Can you believe that?'

'I can believe that a man would do anything for you.'

As he said those words he saw the gulp catch in her throat, and a tear spring to her eyes.

'Oh look, here are the musicians. Come on, let me introduce you!' She was off, like the wind, and within seconds she was standing by a small transit van watching them unload their instruments.

'Hey there, thanks so much for doing this at short notice.'

'No problem Soraya. It's our pleasure. And we've all decided not to charge you for it. We want to be part of the celebration and will happily give our time for free,' Nelson said, kissing Soraya on the cheek.

Simon couldn't believe what he was hearing. Doesn't anyone around here value money?

The musicians began setting up, and Soraya brought in a tray with refreshments.

'I'm going to head upstairs and get changed. Simon, make yourself comfortable in the attic. The bathroom is off the landing to the right of my bedroom. Everything you need is in there.'

Soraya dressed in a long black fitted jersey skirt, and white blouse. She wore ballet pumps, and tied up her hair back into a bun. As she pinned her hair in place she thought about Simon's hands and how they'd gently let her hair down. The symbolism of it didn't escape her. It *was* time to let her hair down. Time to be free. Time to enjoy life a bit more. But was Simon the man to do that with? All he cared about was money! Their life view was too different. It would only be asking for trouble to get into a relationship with a man like that. Soraya caught herself, and laughed at the speed with which her thoughts were racing. He hasn't even kissed you! How can you be thinking about a relationship? Crazy girl!

In the end, she decided that she couldn't let her hair hang down while she was serving food, but she fiddled with a few wisps so that some tendrils hung by her high, defined cheekbones. The effect was immediate, and softened her face. She looked like a woman who wanted to be kissed. *A woman who wanted to be kissed by Simon Beaudin. The* Simon Beaudin. She drizzled a little rose oil onto her wrists, and breathed in the scent. It had always been her favourite, and for a split second she wondered if it was time for a change.

Just as she stepped onto the landing, Simon came out of the bathroom. For a moment, she wondered if it was the same man. His clothes were casual: faded denim jeans tight around his firm buttocks. His long legs were muscular, but it was his chest which caught her eyes. Simon's muscles were firm but lean, and the chest hair visible from between the opened buttons had her legs feeling just a bit too wobbly for someone about to begin waitressing for the night.

'You look...' She wasn't sure what to say. If she

said handsome, he might take that as an invitation.

'I look what?' he asked, hoping to encourage an answer.

'Er, clean. You look clean.'

They both burst out laughing.

'What did you really want to say?' he laughed again, gently placing his hand on her arm.

'Handsome. You look really handsome.' Again, her flushed cheeks were a giveaway. This could be a long night, she thought to herself, but as she walked away Simon reached for her hand. 'You look beautiful, Soraya. I love how you've done your hair.'

There was a skip in her step, as she walked away, and minutes later she was humming softly in the kitchen.

Alice and Murray arrived, dressed in their finest clothes. They may have been together for seventy years, but their love was as fresh as any newlywed. 'Soraya, this is the kindest thing anyone has ever done for us. How can we possibly repay you for your generosity?' Alice asked, reaching out to hold Soraya's hand.

'This is my gift to you. There's nothing to repay. Now, come and make yourselves comfortable. If you have any musical requests, just ask the quartet. I need to head into the kitchen now, but will be with you shortly.'

Simon followed her into the kitchen. 'What can I do to help you?'

'You can be in charge of drinks. We have champagne, vintage red wine and house wine. They're unlikely to want much alcohol, so be sure to let them know we have sparkling or still mineral water, elderflower presse, rosehip wine, apple juice, and ginger ale. Be attentive to their needs, but don't hover.'

'Yes, miss.'

Their eyes caught, and once again they found themselves not wanting to emerge from the bubble of bliss that was created whenever they searched each other for answers. They both relaxed into each other's smile; their hearts beating just that bit faster than a moment ago.

When Simon finally left the kitchen, Soraya found herself thinking once again about her and Simon as a couple. It just couldn't work, she snapped. Instead of feeling happy at Alice and Murray's special day, Soraya found herself feeling irritable that a man as attractive, intelligent and charming as Simon could be so wrong for her. It wasn't fair! If only he wasn't so focused on money. Him and his cold hard cash, she muttered. The thought was hardly out in the air when she had another idea.

Soraya slipped upstairs to her bedroom and pulled out her purse. She took a few seconds to decide, and then removed two fifty dollar notes. Once she was back in the kitchen, she took a cookie cutter from the drawer and placed it on the money. Using a pen, she marked a line around the outside, then cut the paper to reveal a heart made of money. 'That's exactly who he is!' Another thought occurred to her. She glued the two notes to a thick wedge of cardboard, also cut into a heart, and then placed it in the freezer. She'd serve it up to him at breakfast! Cold, hard cash.

Despite the gnawing feeling inside her heart—the push and pull, the yes and the no—she knew, without doubt, that she hoped time would slow down and that the week he was here in Rainbow Valley would never end. It was a silly dream. Life had already taught her that as far as she was concerned there would not be a happily-ever-after. Not now, not ever.

Alice and Murray danced the evening away. Simon and Soraya peeped around the door every few minutes to ensure their guests were happy. Simon stood behind Soraya, his breath warm against her neck. She could feel him close, their clothes almost touching, and she willed him to come closer, even though she knew it was a path neither of them was truly willing to go down. It was all very well being attracted to each other, but relationships needed a more solid foundation than lust. Soraya closed her eyes and breathed him in; his scent was intoxicating. If only time would stand still. This was the closest she'd been to a man in a long time, and it sure felt good. Soraya's skin ached for him to touch her, hold her, and ravish her.

Alice and Murray confessed that they were too tired for a massage or the hot tub, but assured Soraya they'd had the best evening ever. It had been perfect. She showed them to their room, and once they were inside, she danced a silent jig outside their door.

'It's time for me to get some sleep too,' she said to Simon a minute later. 'Feel free to make yourself at home in the kitchen or lounge. If you need extra bedding, you'll find it in a drawer under your bed. Is there anything else you need?'

Simon wanted to say: *Yes, I need you.* Somehow the words seemed ridiculous. How could you need someone you'd only met that morning? He'd already made a fool of himself several times by saying the wrong thing. And what was this need anyway? Healthy lust?

'I'm absolutely fine. Thank you for everything. You're not going to let me kiss you good night, are you?' he smiled, hoping she'd take the bait.

'Probably not.'

Simon marvelled at how bashful she suddenly became, as if she were only fifteen years old.

'That's not a no, then?'

'It's not a yes, either. Good night, Simon. Sleep well.'

Simon carried his bag up the ladder, and placed it by the bed. The first thing he noticed was that she'd removed the photo of herself and her boyfriend. At one level he was touched that she'd been kind enough to consider his feelings, but another part of him was annoyed that he didn't have the pleasure of staring at her beautiful face for the next few hours.

Simon lay back on the bed, and enjoyed watching the stars through the skylight. It was a delightful room, hidden away from the world. What it lacked in floor space, it more than made up for in views. Somehow it reminded him of Soraya: she was delightful, enchanting, beautiful and charming. The world didn't know about her, though. Perhaps that would change once his book was published. For a few moments he found himself toying with the idea of not including House of Hearts in the book. The idea seemed absurd. Simon wrestled with the jealous feelings stirring up from some deep and ancient place within. Simon didn't want to share Soraya. No, he wanted her all to himself. After some time, he fell asleep tormented by the dilemma.

# A Heart Made of Money

Simon rose early, before first light, and headed off to the kitchen to make himself a coffee. He tiptoed across the landing so as not to wake Soraya, and was startled to find she was already in the kitchen making breakfast.

'Good morning. I thought you'd be up soon. Breakfast is ready. Take a seat.'

'Are you naturally an early riser when you don't have guests?'

'Yes, I do a lot of my best work before the Sun rises.'

Something about her body language made him wonder if she'd just shared a deep secret. Simon decided not to pursue it. Today he wanted to make sure he didn't put a foot out of line. After all, he only had six days left with Soraya, and he wanted to make the most of it.

Soraya had prepared him poached eggs with hollandaise sauce and lightly sautéed baby-spinach leaves on heart-shaped English muffins.

'This looks wonderful, Soraya, but you should probably know that your hearts are wasted on me. I'm not looking for love.'

'I'm a giver of hearts, that's what I do Simon. Sorry, but you can't reject it.'

Simon laughed as he watched the smile stretch across her face, enlarging her deeply indented dimples. 'I don't know why I'm drawn to particular hearts, but I follow my intuition. I've never been wrong, apparently, even when the choices make absolutely no sense to me.'

It was his turn to change the subject. 'Will Alice and Murray be staying tonight?'

'No, they've got a huge family party to return

home for. Four generations coming to celebrate their anniversary. Amazing, isn't it? Anyway, I've arranged for them to have breakfast at 8am, and then I've got the day off. Perhaps you could interview me for your book?'

Simon was about to say something, and then she continued.

'But I do have a couple of errands. I need to pick up some hearts from Barnaby. We can walk there, if you like. It's along the river. It's beautiful this time of year.'

'Sounds great!' Simon ate his breakfast, wondering how an egg could taste so good. Was he hungrier than usual?

Soraya pottered around her tiny kitchen for a while, and then said, 'Everyone gets heart-shaped toast or muffins when they stay. I didn't do it especially for you. You're cute, but you're not *that* cute!' she laughed as she stood there, hands on hips.

'Soraya, I was only kidding about not giving me a heart. If you want to give me one, then you're more than welcome. I will respect whatever choice you make. I promise.'

How long would it take him to eat his words? Would he eat them as quickly as he'd swallowed his eggs?

'Really?'

'Yes, of course.'

'Okay. Close your eyes.'

'What?'

'You heard me: close your eyes.'

Simon obliged, smiling at the possibilities before him.

Soraya quietly opened the freezer door and pulled out his cold, hard cash.

'Keep your eyes closed,' she whispered, holding one of his hands in hers, and then placed the frozen heart on his palm.

'What the hell is that?' he yelled as the shock of cold sent sharp pangs into his hand. As his eyes opened and he took in the sight before him, his conscious mind started to make the associations. 'Funny, Soraya. Very funny. Do you really see me like this? Do you think I don't care about things or people? Do you think I'm hard hearted? Do you think I'm not capable of...' He didn't finish his sentence. Simon suddenly felt like a teenager having a tantrum, and he quickly brought his emotions back under control.

'Don't let me stop you talking, Mr Beaudin.'

'I'm more than capable of love, Soraya. Just because I pursue a career involving money, it doesn't mean that I'm cold. You've got me all wrong. The heart-shaped muffins, I'll take, but not this. It's not who I am.'

Simon was quite clear that he'd had the last word on the matter, but when she simply responded with 'prove it', he was left dumbstruck.

'How? How do you want me to prove it?' Simon was exasperated. This was not how he wanted the day to start.

'Show me your heart.' Soraya said.

What did she want from him? What did she expect from him?

'Simon, show me that there is more to you and more to your life than money. Show me this other side of you.'

'Just who is interviewing whom?' he said, letting his anger dissipate.

They finished the rest of their breakfast in silence, and then Simon joined her in the restaurant kitchen to prepare a meal for Murray and Alice. After breakfast, there were teary goodbyes and promises of a return visit, and then Soraya and Simon found themselves standing on the roadside in front of House of Hearts.

'I'm sorry if I was snappy earlier, but Soraya, there is a man underneath the journalist.'

'I know,' she whispered softly. 'Let me close up the house and shop, and we can take a walk to Barnaby's workshop.'

# The Landowner

They walked in pleasurable silence for several minutes, with Simon taking in the view before him. To his mind, everything about her was gorgeous. Soraya, at five foot seven, had long, toned legs. She strode purposefully along the river's edge. From time to time their eyes met, and they smiled without saying a word.

Simon adored the slight gap between her front teeth, and how her high cheekbones became even more exaggerated whenever she smiled. Her pert nose nestled between her perfectly symmetrical chocolate-brown eyes.

Simon wanted to hear her voice again, and the sound of her laughter.

'This must be private land we're walking on. Do you have permission to be here?'

'It is private land.'

'Do you have the owner's permission?' he asked again.

'Yes,' she smiled. 'I do. I'm the owner.'

'Oh. I had no idea. Did you inherit?'

'So many questions, Mr Beaudin. No, I did not inherit the land. I bought it. I earned every last penny. No loans, no gifts, no grants. I worked, and I rewarded myself with an investment. Because it's adjacent to my home, it greatly increases the value of both properties. I imagine that must be music to your ears,' she said, with just a hint of sarcasm. 'You might think I'm just some romance-obsessed woman without much going on upstairs, but I'm as business savvy as any other shop owner in town.'

Simon looked a little bamboozled. 'How long have you had House of Hearts?'

'Five years,' she said matter of factly, brushing her hand against the bark of an oak tree.

'And when did you buy the land?' he queried, already entering into mathematical equations.

Soraya enlarged her eyes as if to say 'enough with the questions already', but then chose to answer him. 'I bought it four years ago.'

'So you earned enough in the space of a year to buy this? How many acres do you have?'

'Fifty five acres.'

'That must have cost...'

'What, you're a realtor, too?' she asked, nipping his last comment before he finished. 'I love it along here at this time of the year. Fall is the prettiest season, don't you think?'

Simon didn't answer her seasonal query, but instead said 'I have quite a keen interest in property investment, as it happens. How much does House of Hearts bring in?' Simon was trying to get his thoughts around how a small-town business could generate the income necessary to purchase a property like this.

'Hey you,' she laughed. 'You're not interviewing me now. You're meant to be walking with me to Barnaby's. Let's talk about something else.'

The morning mist had almost burnt off in the sunshine, and the clear day accentuated the mustard, scarlet and tan leaves. Simon reached for her hand and they continued their walk that Autumn day, side by side.

'Barnaby lives on the land. We have a deal: he can live in his gypsy wagon here for free, and I get a discount on the heart pieces that he whittles for me. He's a bit of a hermit, really, and likes being alone up here with his horses.'

They entered a clearing near the edge of the woodland, and found Barnaby squatting by his campfire and preparing a pot of tea.

'Just in time,' he smiled, beckoning them over. He stood up, his curly hair wild and unwashed, and leaned forward to hug Soraya.

Simon felt a pang inside that he couldn't quite identify. It wasn't because the woodturner left shavings on Soraya's pretty blouse, it was something else. Something unfamiliar. It was a feeling that made him want to take her straight home.

'Barnaby, this is Simon. He's in the valley for a few days on business. I thought I'd bring him here for a look around.'

'Hi buddy, make yourself comfortable. Tea?'

After their drinks, Barnaby stepped up into his gypsy wagon, and brought out a box containing his latest creations. 'Hope you like these, Soraya. As per usual, each item is one of a kind.'

'Oh Barnaby, they're just lovely!'

'These are amazing,' Simon added. 'Do you supply other businesses?'

Soraya shot him a look. 'Get out of interview mode, Simon. This place is Barnaby's retreat.'

'I don't mind answering. I make spoons and dishes to sell at the Saturday market, but the hearts are only for Soraya.'

'So your hearts are exclusive to House of Hearts?'

'Yes,' Barnaby said proudly.

Simon mentally filed the rest of the conversation away in his mind. He filed it under: Soraya. *Beautiful* Soraya.

They returned to House of Hearts in time for lunch. 'I'll just make us a bite to eat, and then we can do the interview, if you like,' Soraya offered, closing the door behind them.

'Let's eat in the restaurant.' Simon caught her hand, and turned Soraya around to face him.

'No. We can't do that. Only lovers dine there.' Her refusal was polite, but firm.

'I'd like to dine there with you...to get a feel of it for my chapter on this place. Please.'

'It won't be the same. You don't understand the magic of the place, Simon. We can't possibly eat there. It's infused with essential oils to enhance intimacy.'

'Oh, I'm quite aware of the effect of that room. I would like to have lunch with you there, if I may. I like the idea of experiencing that room with you, and you alone. Don't be scared of me, Soraya.'

'I'm not...I'm not *scared*. I just... Never mind. Sure. We can eat there.'

He could tell that she was not at all happy about the prospect of sharing such an intimate lovers' retreat with him.

Simon followed her to the kitchen, and helped prepare lunch. In no time at all, they were seated in the restaurant dining on grilled smoky eggplant, nutty chickpeas and earthy walnuts. Simon poured a glass of mellow red wine. 'May I start the interview now?' he asked, setting up the Dictaphone to record their conversation.

'Sure,' she said.

Simon had already noticed that she'd been avoiding eye contact since the moment they sat down together.

'You obviously run a successful business that

has not only survived but appears to have thrived during the recession. What business advice would you give?' he asked. Even he was surprised by how formal he suddenly sounded. It was as if he'd slipped completely into journalist mode, and the informality of the morning's walk through the woods just evaporated. Would she engage in conversation with *this* Simon when it was clear that she wanted the other one: the man who laughed, and whose smile melted her heart. The one who made her feel like a woman.

'Firstly, my business *has* thrived. It's not just an appearance,' she said, putting him firmly in his place. 'As for business advice, what works for me is working minimal hours. So many men become workaholics and think you have to work fourteen-hour days, seven days a week. But actually, less is more. What's important is to have plenty of free time to balance out the work. Business decisions are more effective when we do them with a clear head. I like afternoon naps and walks in the woods and to cook. I do all this myself; I have no staff, so I need hours to suit my lifestyle. I work five days a week from 10am to 2pm, and on Saturdays from 9am to noon. Most weekends I have someone stay in the B&B, but that's not too time consuming as the honeymooners tend to want to be alone.'

'So you've mastered the four-hour work day?'

'This is more than a business, Simon; this is a way of life. It's simple: do what you love and the money will come. Money is love.'

'What does *that* mean?' he asked, incredulous that the two words were not only being used in the same sentence, but that Soraya somehow believed they were interchangeable.

They might well have been in her fantasy imagination, but not in the real world. Not in Simon's world.

'Contrary to what most people think, money isn't the root of all evil. Humans are. Money is just paper. But, in our world, we have it elevated to God-like status.'

'Money changes lives, Soraya. How could you even think otherwise?'

'Of course it changes lives, but if you don't follow your heart you lead a compromised life…and then what is the point of all that cash?'

Simon continued with dozens of questions even when it was obvious that she was becoming exhausted.

'So what is it that drives you, if it's not money?'

'Did you really just ask me that question?' Soraya stood up and walked out of the restaurant.

*What did I say this time?* Simon muttered after she'd vanished.

In a few short seconds she returned with a small plate, and offered him a heart-shaped dark Belgian chocolate filled with rose cream.

'Some people are frantically looking for love. What I offer is a shop that has them focusing more on themselves. People expect someone to come along and fill the empty hole inside them, but that never works. We have to be happy and complete within ourselves.'

This time she did make eye contact. How could someone so wrong for him be so darn attractive? It was starting to irritate him now.

'So you think people should just get on with their lives instead of actively looking for love?'

'Yes. I firmly believe that the person you're looking for is also looking for you. We're all connected by an invisible thread. Meeting your soulmate is inevitable, but if you take second best you won't be available when they come along.'

Simon shook his head, wondering where she got her crazy ideas from.

They finished eating, and then Soraya heard a knock at the front door.

'Customers on a Sunday?' he asked.

'No, that'll be my sister, Santana. She's a florist, and delivers roses every few days.'

'Can I meet her?' Simon asked, curious to learn more about Soraya and her family.

'That's not necessary. You stay here. I'll be back in a minute.'

Before he had time to argue, she was gone. Simon wiped his mouth with a napkin, and ten seconds later was jolted by the sound of Soraya screaming. Without a second's hesitation, he raced out of the restaurant, and saw her lying, like a crumpled fairy, at the bottom of the stairs.

'Don't move,' he yelled, running, two steps at a time, to meet her. As he reached the bottom of the stairs, he was shocked to see the bone in her lower leg puncturing her skin. Soraya was drifting in and out of consciousness.

Loud knocking forced him to look up. Torn between two people, he raced over and unlatched the door, and was quickly back at Soraya's side.

'She needs an ambulance. Here, use my phone,' he said, reaching into his back pocket. 'I'm Simon, by the way.'

'Santana, I'm Soraya's sister,' she said, placing a metal bucket of roses down on the floor. 'What happened?'

'She must have tripped.'

'Hi, we need an ambulance straight away to House of Hearts, main street, Rainbow Valley. Looks like a broken leg. Patient is unconscious. Hurry, please. Thank you.' Her voice was shaky, as tears slipped from her eyes.

Santana passed the phone back to him, and held Soraya's hand. 'Sis, can you hear me? Soraya, wake up.'

'Are you twins?' Simon asked, astonished at the similarities.

'Yes, I'm older by three minutes. Not that you'd know it. She always was the bossy one.'

They shared a gentle laugh, which helped to diffuse some of the tension, and continued to call Soraya's name until they heard the siren approaching.

'I'll grab the keys and lock up,' Santana said. 'Are you and your wife staying in the B&B upstairs?'

'No. I'm not married. But I am staying upstairs.'

'Oh. Are you and…Never mind, it was a silly question.'

Two paramedics came in through the front door, the Tibetan bells ringing as they did so.

'She fell down the stairs,' Santana said. 'Will she be okay?'

The men squatted down beside Soraya, and within a minute she was regaining consciousness. 'San,' she said. 'My leg!' and screamed. 'It hurts!'

'We're just giving you something now for the pain, Miss,' a paramedic said, trying to reassure her. 'My name is John. I'll be with you in the back of the ambulance. I just need you to keep calm. If you can, try and breathe deeply. It will help you to stay conscious.'

Simon reached forward and held Soraya's hand. 'They'll have you to the hospital in no time.'

'Simon, I'm so sorry. We'll just have to postpone the rest of the…aggggh.' She screamed again.

'Just give it a few more seconds for the pain relief to register. You'll be comfortable soon,' John said.

'Santana, can you wait here until Simon has packed his things and then lock up afterwards?'

'Sure I can, sis. Then I'll be straight down to the hospital.'

'I'm not going anywhere, Soraya. You've just broken your leg. How do you think you're going to manage all those flights of stairs when you get back home?'

'What?'

'You can't stay here. You'll have to come back to my place.' Simon spoke firmly, as if it was the only available solution to her dilemma.

Santana looked at him in disbelief. 'Let's go back a few seconds. I'm lost. How do you know each other? Are you two dating? Soraya, why haven't you told me any of this?'

'There's nothing to tell. Simon is…'

'We're just going to put you on the stretcher now,' the paramedic informed her. 'Try not to move. Let us do the moving for you.'

He turned to Santana and Simon and said 'She'll be in the ER for several hours. They're real busy down there today. Halloween next week, and lots of knife wounds. I suggest you bring a book to read.'

'Simon, thanks for your help, but I can look after my sister.'

'I have no doubt about that at all. I'm here, so I'd like to do what I can. Shall I drive you, or would you like to go in the ambulance?'

'Come with me, San.'

Simon could read her like a book: she was terrified of leaving them alone together in case Simon dug around too much in her past and had Santana relaying every last event of Soraya's life.

The paramedic was right. ER was mayhem. Santana and Simon found each other in the waiting room.

*What a gentleman,* she thought to herself when he came towards her carrying two cups of coffee.

'Thanks, I needed that. I was only coming by with her roses. Hadn't planned to stay. That'll teach me for being a slack sister!'

They sat in silence for some time until Santana couldn't keep her thoughts to herself anymore.

'Don't break Soraya's heart. No one in this town could bear it,' she advised gently as she looked down into her coffee.

'What's that supposed to mean?' he asked, shocked at the underlying accusatory tone.

'If you care for her, like the look in your eyes says you do, then make sure that you're Mr Third Time Lucky.'

'Third time? I have no idea what you're talking about. I don't know the first thing about Soraya's love life. Whenever I try and broach the subject, she steers me well away. If there's something I should know, then please tell me.'

'It's not my place. I'll say this, though: she might dish out hearts to everyone who comes through that front door, but no one needs one more than she does. If you can give her that, then you have my blessing. If you plan to break it, then I never want to see you again!'

'So feistiness runs in the family, then?' he said

softly, his smile disarming her just as easily as it had done to her sister.

'You better believe it.' From that moment on, they understood each other much better.

'She won't be able to manage those stairs. Has she got anyone she can call in to run the shop?'

'She'll probably just close it for a few weeks.'

'What about cash flow?'

Santana laughed. 'Soraya's wealthy. Don't let her little floral dresses and bare feet fool you. That woman earns money faster than anyone else in my world. "Shrewd Business Woman" are her three middle names.'

'From selling hearts?' Simon was miffed. 'But she gives so many of them away!'

'Look, she could get someone in, but it wouldn't be the same. That shop needs the Soraya touch. I filled in for a few weeks once, and even though we look alike, it just wasn't the same. Soraya brings something unique to the place. It's a bit like that old saying: we teach best what we need to learn. Shutting it is the best option.'

Two hours and three cups of instant coffee later, they finally saw Soraya come hobbling towards them. 'Six weeks! Six weeks on crutches. Can you believe it?'

'It'll zip by, sis. I'll get you all comfortable and set up in that lovely lounge of yours. You could do with a little holiday.'

'I'm not closing the shop, if that's what you're thinking.'

Santana and Simon looked at each other. It wasn't worth arguing. Not yet, at least. They'd wait until she tried the stairs, and then they'd offer their support.

'I can do this!' Soraya insisted as she took the first steps onto the verandah of House of Hearts. The pain was evident. Simon passed the crutches to Santana, and in one quick swoop lifted Soraya into his arms. 'Don't even think of arguing. You're outnumbered.'

Simon carried her upstairs, and Santana made them each a cup of tea and cobbled a sandwich from various leftovers in the fridge.

'We have to be realistic, Ray...this place isn't suitable for a person with a broken leg. You're coming back to my place. Adam and I can job share until you've found your feet. No pun intended.'

'No,' she replied, shaking her head furiously.

'My home doesn't have stairs, and I'm working from there for a few months, so why not come back with me?' Simon said, resting his hand on hers tenderly.

'Because I don't know you!' Soraya insisted.

'Yes, but you will know me by the time your leg is better.'

Soraya turned away so she didn't get caught up in his dazzling smile. She needed to be strong, and stand her ground. This was her home, and that's where she was staying. Damn the way his smile had a way of making her forget her own name!

'Where do you live?' Santana asked him.

'New York.'

'But that's four hours away!' She calmed down a little, and then continued. 'You can really do this? She could stay with you?'

'Excuse me people, I'm in the room. Don't I get a say?'

'No,' they said in unison, not even turning to look in her direction.

Santana pulled out her business card: *Country Basket Florists*. 'You call me if she needs anything. Anything at all.'

'I promise,' Simon said calmly, his deep voice soothing her. Soothing both of them.

'I don't believe this,' Soraya said. 'I don't believe this at all. Santana, you're not seriously going to let a strange man take me to his home?'

'Well, he looks pretty harmless,' Santana laughed. 'It's perfect, really. I get to continue interviewing you for the book, and you can't run away to a customer or to the oven. Isn't that what they call win-win?'

'You're loving this, aren't you?' Soraya said, feeling somewhat exasperated.

'It's too late to drive back tonight. We'll go in the morning. What can I do to help you get ready for bed?'

From alabaster to crimson in three seconds. That's all it took for her face to register what he'd said: bed. It was such a simple word, but when he said it her mind immediately thought in images: she wondered what it would be like to make love with Simon Beaudin. *The* Simon Beaudin.

'I can manage, thanks.'

'Well, I best be on my way. Are you sure you're going to be okay, sis?' Santana asked one final time.

'Yes, I think so.'

'I'll take the spare key and collect your mail and water your plants.' Then she turned to Simon. 'Look after her.'

He knew exactly what she meant, and wasn't about to argue. Simon led her out to the front door. 'I have no intention of hurting your sister,' he said when he was out of earshot. 'My relationship is strictly professional. It suits me to have her at my home. I can multitask, editing other parts of my book, and interview her when she's awake and comfortable. It also means I'm there if she needs help.'

'If you say so,' Santana said, not entirely trusting her sister's heart into a man's hands but unable to think of a better solution.

Simon felt relieved to walk back up the stairs. If he thought he'd met his match with Soraya, he'd most definitely met it with Santana. What a pair!


Soraya slept fitfully, each physical movement taken hostage by her plastered leg, and each thought and lucid dream waylaid by the image of Simon Beaudin in the attic. She was dreading going to the toilet, and how was she going to have a shower?

At 6am, Simon knocked lightly on her bedroom door. 'I've brought you breakfast.'

'Come in.' She had hoped to brush her hair and wash her face before she saw him, but it was too late now. Too late for everything.

'Your hair is looking good,' he smiled, then pressed the breakfast tray onto her lap. 'I'll help you shower,' he said matter-of-factly.

'No you will not!'

'Soraya, you won't manage it on your own. You could risk breaking your other leg.'

'I'm prepared to take that risk.'

'Are you always so stubborn?'

'I'm…the breakfast looks lovely, thank you.'

As she took a mouthful of the sautéed mushrooms, Simon laughed to see the look on her face. '

You can cook?' she said, shocked to her core.

'Of course I can cook. Did you think I ate out every night of the week?'

'I don't know what I thought, but…Never mind. Have you eaten?'

'I have. We're going to have fun, you and I. I think we'll get to know each other real well over the next month or so.' And that smile: the one that made her belly flip over every single time, how was she going to live with that? 'I've made a notice for the front door. All we need to do is pack you a case, and then we're good to go.'

Simon wandered over to her drawers, and began taking items of underwear from them.

'What are you doing?' she gasped. 'That's private. That's my underwear!'

'Packing. Do you have a preference for which underwear? The safe ones: cotton, or the risky ones: lace?'

'Cotton, thank you! Look, give me five minutes and I'll pack those things myself.'

'Just helping the process. Don't bother yourself. Finish your breakfast.'

By the time her mushrooms were eaten, Simon had returned with two plastic garbage bags and some string. He placed two towels on the bed and said, 'Right, let's get this plaster covered and get you into the shower.'

'I can do this!'

'Oh, I'm sure you can do anything that you set your mind to, Soraya, but I promised your sister that I'd look after you, and that's what I'm doing. Let me help you out of bed.'

'Simon, you might have a nationwide fan base, and have women dropping on their knees in front of you, but that doesn't mean you can just come in here and watch me get naked.'

'Actually, it's an international fan base, but you're right: let's be realistic here, though, do you really think I'll be turned on by the sight of a naked lady hobbling about in a leg plaster?'

'How would I know what turns you on?'

'I'll just pretend you're my little sister, if it makes you feel better.'

'The thought of you watching your sister naked does not make me feel better.'

'Do you want a shower or not?'

'Of course I do! Simon, just let me do this on my own.'

'No. Now stop arguing. It's getting weary.'

It took about seven minutes for Simon to secure the plastic bags in such a way that her plaster would remain safe from the water. Not that Soraya was counting the minutes, but sitting on her bed, naked, ensured it was the longest seven minutes of her life. Well, almost.

As she stood up, he linked his arm in hers. 'Leave the crutches, I'll walk you in.'

Reluctant, at first, she leant on Simon, and allowed him to help her into the shower. Within seconds, steam swirled through the room providing pseudo protection from his lingering eyes.

Though he behaved like a gentleman, she could feel him taking in every last inch of her body. Was he imagining what it would be like to touch her? The thought of it sent a shiver up her spine.

Soraya heard him breathe in deeply. Was he controlling his pulse? Perhaps he was breathing in her rose scent? Whatever it was, it was clear that he was trying to slow down time and make every second count.

'I can probably manage now,' she insisted, but he dismissed the notion.

'I'll wash your hair. Turn around.'

Without uttering another word, she surrendered to her fate. It actually felt good to have him wash her hair. It had been such a long afternoon in the ER yesterday, followed by a fitful sleep last night. All the tension evaporated as he massaged her scalp with deep, slow moves.

'Have you done this before?' she asked.

'Washed the hair of a woman with a broken leg? No, this is a first.'

'You're rather skilled at it.'

'Tell me something. Am I growing on you, Soraya?'

She didn't say anything, and became aware of his hands leaving her head, and touching her shoulders.

'You're tense,' he whispered, and began rubbing her neck, shoulders and arms. 'I'm not going to hurt you. I'm trying to help you. Stop resisting me. You might just enjoy yourself.'

'And then what?' she asked, closing her eyes.

'What do you mean?'

'What happens after I finish enjoying myself? Then what?'

'Are you wanting a promise of some sort?'

Simon had no room in his life for a relationship. It would be ludicrous to promise anything, or to hint of a future. They barely knew each other. Bringing her to his home was an act of kindness, but it came with an ulterior motive: he wanted to get his book finished, and there was more chance of that happening well away from House of Hearts. And if he was honest, the feel of a gorgeous woman under his hands, and in his bed, hadn't escaped his thoughts. It had been a while since he'd enjoyed that particular pleasure. But long term? No. His life was not designed for such luxury. One thing was clear: Soraya Juniper was not a one-night-stand sort of woman.

Simon chose not to continue the conversation, but instead picked up the jasmine-scented soap and began washing her back.

'How does that feel?' he asked after hearing an involuntary sigh escape her lips.

'Great, actually.'

'And this?'

Soraya didn't answer with words. Simon steadied her as she began to sway.

'Seems to me like you've been neglected, Soraya. Let's see what we can do to change that.' Simon gently turned her around to face him, and his hands slid down to her hips.

'You're getting wet,' she whispered.

'Yes. Best take my clothes off then.'

Soraya gasped.

'No! It's bad enough that I'm naked.'

'What do you think is going to happen, Soraya?'

'Well, it's just that...'

'Go on. I'm listening.'

'I just don't think it's a good idea.'

'That's a shame. I do.' Simon casually removed his shirt. When she averted her eyes, it was all he could do to not start laughing.

'Soraya, you're not fifteen. There's no need to be coy!'

'I'm not coy! Standing in the shower, naked, with a man I barely know is...'

'Sexy, don't you think?'

'With a leg in plaster?'

'That plaster is the last thing I'm thinking of right now.' He stepped, buck naked, under the shower spray and then stood back and moved Soraya in front of him. Let me wash your front. Don't argue. I'm already wet, so let me finish what I started.'

At first, she closed her eyes, taking in the sensations. She was slightly alarmed at how darn good it felt to be held by him. It was such a vulnerable, intimate situation to be in. Try as she might, she couldn't remember a time in her life when she felt so damn exposed. What hope did she have of keeping him at arm's length? Then Soraya allowed herself the indescribable pleasure of looking at him. As she did so, she wanted to run her fingers through his hair, and kiss his stubbled jaw. The unshaven look brought out deep primal urges within her, feelings she'd not had in years. It was unnerving. How could a man who was so wrong for her be so irresistible? She knew, however, that she did have to resist. Simon Beaudin might have been too good looking and charming for his own good, but she had the strength to say "no".

'I appreciate everything you're doing, and I really get the ulterior-motive thing you've got going on with getting your book finished, but I'm not someone you can pick up, play with, and then let go of. Don't do that to me.'

Simon knew she was right. Everything about the situation was wrong. Of course he wanted to make love to her, and truth be told, he could see her being in his life for a little while, but not forever. The latter was just ridiculous. Career and intimate relationships weren't happy bedfellows. And besides, she was not the sort of person to fit into his world.

'What exactly is it that you think I'm going to do, Soraya?'

'I don't know what's going on in your head, but I feel vulnerable and completely out of my comfort zone. I don't need to come to New York. I'll manage just fine on my own. Really. If you're so concerned about finishing the interview, perhaps we can video call?'

'No, I'd rather interview you in person.'

His hands tenderly traced her hips, and then washed her belly. Simon squatted down to wash her unplastered leg but couldn't help notice that she flushed and had to shut her eyes. Now his hand was on the inside of her upper thigh, warm and slippery from the soap, and just an inch away from the top of her legs; he sensed that she found it almost impossible to stand up.

The woman might have been putty in his hands, but he wasn't a complete scoundrel. As tempting as it was to carry her to bed and make love to her, the time wasn't right.

'I'll grab a towel,' he said softly, his voice gravelly with desire. For the next minute or so, he dried her, slowly absorbing the moisture from her tanned skin. Their eyes were in constant contact, and although she looked like a rabbit in headlights, Simon hoped that as each moment passed she'd come to a place of feeling safe around him. That time hadn't come yet.

'Come and sit on the bed, and I'll undo the plastic from your leg.'

'Simon?'

'Yes?'

'Are you going to shower me every day?'

'That's the plan. Do you have any objections?'

'Well, yes, actually. I don't think I can go through that again. It was torture.'

'Go through what?'

It was cruel to even ask her; he knew exactly what she meant, and the truth was he loved every second of it. Damn it, she was beautiful, and she was turned on by him. The next six weeks sure were going to be fun!

'Never mind, but I think I need to find a way to be more independent with or without this blasted cast on my leg.'

'So, I've packed your bag. Shall we go?'

'Actually, I need a few things from the loft. Would you mind?'

'Sure, what do you want?'

'Laptop, hard drive, printer.'

'You're meant to be resting. You can use my printer and hard drive. I've probably even got a spare laptop if you want to surf the net.'

'No, I'm good. I'd like my own laptop, thanks.'

'Fine. Wait here.'

'I'm not going to be climbing that ladder any time soon, Simon. Actually, while you're there, there's a portable file I'd like. It's under the desk.'

'Anything else?' he chuckled. 'I won't need a gym workout after going up and down there four or five times.'

'No, that's all. Oh, and some pens. One of each color.'

'Pens it is.'

'Thanks.'

Simon walked away, his hair still damp from the shower. It was all Soraya could do to think straight. Six weeks, she thought to herself. Six weeks?

# New York City

Despite the sign on the front door letting customers know the shop was closed until further notice due to injury, a loud and persistent knock had Simon heading down there, taking two steps at a time.

'Don't trip!' Soraya called out, clenching her teeth as she waited for the sound of catastrophe. The Tibetan bells rang out, and she sighed with relief.

Simon took hold of a large parcel, and signed the delivery note. Several minutes later, when he helped Soraya down the stairs, she asked if he could wait in the car while she just checked the contents.

'It's fine, I can wait here for you. There's no hurry.'

What is she up to?, he wondered when her body language revealed that she was quite keen to open the box on her own.

Soraya cut through the tape and let out an excited squeal as she pulled out a book.

'What's so exciting?' he asked.

'Nothing.'

'You don't react like that to nothing.'

'Latest release. Can you help me get them onto the shelves? I know I can't sell them till I get back, but it would make me feel better if they were out of the box.'

Simon carried the box to the corner of the shop which stocked romance novels.

'Hang on,' he said, 'All these books, and the ones on the shelves, are by the same author.'

'Yeah, Ashley Starr. She's good!'

'Why don't you stock other writers?'

'No need. She's a bestseller. No point stocking writers who don't sell as well. Don't you agree?'

Simon laughed.

Perhaps she was an astute business woman after all.

'Are you ready now?'

'As I'll ever be.'

'Are you taking a copy of the book to read?'

'No.'

'But I thought she was good?'

'She is. She's the best. I can catch up when I get back.'

With her leg stuck straight out in front of her, the four-hour road trip seemed more like forty hours. The aerodynamic brilliance of Simon's R8 Spyder Audi wasn't lost on her, nor was the finely crafted interior. It's just that it was hard to sit in a ladylike way or to make herself comfortable. It could have been worse though; she could have been on a bus. Or, she thought to herself ruefully, climbing the sets of stairs at House of Hearts. Soraya allowed herself to feel grateful for Simon's kindness. Although he wanted an interview, he didn't have to take her to his home.

They chatted lightly for some time, before she decided to put the seat back and take a nap. Her dreams were all of Simon. When she awoke a couple of hours later, he was singing along to the song on the radio: Johnny Lee's *Looking For Love In All The Wrong Places*.

'Have you been looking for love in all the wrong places?' Soraya asked.

'It's just a song! Don't read anything into it!' he said, laughing it off.

'You were singing it with such gusto.'

'It's a country song. That's the only way they can be sung. How did you sleep?'

'Fine, I guess.'

'We'll be home in about half an hour,' he said, reading the Audi's navigation with real-time traffic updates. 'This is the worst part. At least it's not rush hour.'

'This isn't rush hour?'

'Have you been to New York before?'

'Not for years. We tend to go to Boston instead.'

'Is there anything you'd like to do while you're here? I can hire a wheelchair.'

'You're working, remember? I'll be just fine on the sofa, thanks.'

'I'm sure we can both make a bit of time for some leisure. Besides, you're a guest in my town and I'd like to treat you.'

It never occurred to Soraya that Simon would live in such a luxurious home. The truth was that she hadn't given it much thought. There were too many other things to consider. It was obvious from his clothing and his car that he was wealthy, but his penthouse went way beyond wealth.

Despite being located in the heart of busy New York, she immediately had a sense of being far away from the noise and the crowds. The first thing which struck her was the high ceilings, and the floor-to-ceiling windows. She stood by the doors of the terrace, taking in the view of the city skyline. They were on the forty-sixth floor.

'I've never been in such a place,' Soraya said softly, admiring the gracious design and layout. The entrance gallery featured marble floors and mahogany panels. The open-plan library boasted Brazilian rosewood, and the modern kitchen was a blend of bamboo, textured glass and forest-green lacquer.

'It feels like you can see the whole city from here.'

'You more or less can: that's midtown Manhattan,' he said, pointing, 'and the Empire State Building, downtown, the Hudson River, and the East River bridges.'

'Do you entertain a lot?' she asked, breathing in the ambience of the dining area. It was the perfect place to have guests.

'Mostly small business meetings. I spend a lot of my time around people. At night, I prefer my own company.'

'Are you naturally a loner?'

'I have two distinct sides to my nature. Yes, I'm quite a loner. That is, I like my own company. But I also like to socialise. Most of my socialising comes through work, so I don't tend to carry it into my personal life.'

Simon helped her along to the other rooms: the bathroom with its marble bath and fireplace, and the main bedroom.

Soraya reached down and felt the bed, and marvelled at the Bellino Italian linen. The man had style!

'Your world is so different to mine. I'm not surprised you haven't been able to take my business seriously.'

'You're wrong, actually. I do take your business skills seriously. Soraya, I admire your brain and your ability to take a niche market and make it grow. The more I've thought about it, I've come to realise House of Hearts is a brilliant chapter for my book. It's unexpected, and it will give entrepreneurs a lot to think about. Despite working minimal hours, you've created a model framework. Business people can learn a lot from you.'

'Where's my room?' she asked, changing the subject. 'Or am I sleeping on the sofa?'

'My bed is large enough for both of us. It's best if you're nearby so I can help you if you need anything in the night.'

'Simon.'

'Soraya. You're not about to argue, are you?'

'Yes, I am. Simon…'

'Save it. I'm here to look after you. I promise not to take advantage of you or do anything you don't want me to do. Let's get you comfortable in the lounge. I'll order up some food as the kitchen's a bit empty.'


Simon set up his Dictaphone, and began the interview while they were eating a late lunch. Soraya couldn't speak. The food was just so delicious that she kept raising her hand to say 'not yet'. He'd ordered them both Greek feta baked with sweet capsicum, onion, herbs and olive oil served with fresh salad leaves.

'No dessert until you've answered some questions,' he laughed. 'I want to make the most of every minute that you're here. I believe House of Hearts will be the feature of the book.'

'The unique selling point?'

'Yes, you could put it that way.'

'Ironic that someone as wealthy as you would make money from someone like me.'

'Don't be sceptical, Soraya. Now, tell me, what inspired the business woman in you?'

'Simon, let me remind you that I didn't go into House of Hearts to make money. That was not and will never be my purpose. Like the rainbows in Rainbow Valley, we're all believers, deep down, in a pot of gold. Is it so wrong to want someone to cherish us? When I give someone a heart, or when they buy one, they're tapping into something about themselves. Rather than looking outward, they're looking within. We don't see things as they are, but as we are. That's the message of the shop.'

'Yes, but how do you make money?'

Soraya was exasperated.

'Have you been listening to anything I've said? You and your money! Would you like to look at my annual accounts? Simon, people are always searching for love. That's what my trade is about.'

'Okay, who were your early influences?' It was time to change tack. It was clear that she was not going to give him what he was looking for: a magical formula for business success.

'My parents taught me the value of things, not the price. I believe that is essential in business. You're not selling a product but something of value. When that becomes your goal, and the reason you go to work each day, then you automatically draw the income towards you.'

The waiter arrived with dessert. 'I can't eat like this if I'm not exercising, Simon. I'll blow up like a balloon.'

'Today, you can eat. Tomorrow, you can exercise.'

Soraya laughed at the ridiculousness of it, but found her resolve wane rapidly as she began to savour apples pan fried in caramel sauce and served with cinnamon crème fraîche.

'I'm going to type up some notes. Will you be comfortable here or would you like to go to the bedroom?'

'I'm perfectly fine on the sofa, thanks. Perhaps you can bring my laptop over?'

'Internet withdrawal already? Are you a closet social-media addict?'

Soraya laughed it off. Simon could think whatever he liked. What she did on her laptop was none of his business. Not now, not ever.

Once Soraya was set up and organised, Simon left her to go into his writing studio. The room had views across the Hudson, and was immaculately designed. Nothing was out of place. For the first few minutes, he sat down and just breathed in the view: the one he'd worked so hard for. Now that he was back here, he realised how much he'd missed his penthouse. He actually hadn't given it much thought when he was tucked up in Soraya's attic.

Was Soraya Juniper really in his penthouse? As he looked back over the past few days, he shook his head in disbelief.

'Enough, already,' he said, and turned his Dictaphone on to type up the conversation.

*House of Hearts*, he typed, and put in the day's date. He didn't notice it straight away, but soon realised he was not typing up what she was saying. Her voice lulled him to some place far away from the world of finance. Poetic words were coming to him, teasing at the corners of his mind: the fall of her hair, the slope of her nose, her rose-scented trail as she walked across the room. The soft way she smiled, and her lyrical laughter.

'Get a grip,' he told himself, but it was no use; he was in no state to write this chapter. Simon gave his imagination free flow, and the words which came out felt like the first lines of a novel. 'Stupid man,' he scoffed, but laughed as the words spilled onto the blank screen. 'Ten minutes,' he told himself, 'and then you get back to work! Real writing.'

Three hours passed, and with that the first chapter of a novel came into life. 'Where the hell did that come from?' Simon asked himself. For a time, he stood at the window. For seven years he'd seen that view, and not once, not a single time, had he ever had the urge to write fiction. What was that woman doing to him? Simon Beaudin had a name to uphold: he was the definitive voice of finance not just across America, but also throughout the Asian and Southern Hemisphere markets. This was no time to unravel the life he knew. He was comfortable. More than comfortable. A woman would undo everything he'd worked so hard for.

A light tap at the door trawled him away from his fantasies. And that's all they were, he told himself: fantasies. Soraya was a beautiful woman, but they had zero in common. Any thoughts about them having a relationship were ludicrous. Time to get back to reality.

'Soraya, sorry to leave you alone for so long,' he said apologetically.

'That's fine. Just wanted to check you were okay!'

'Perfectly fine. Thank you. Shall we go out for dinner?'

'With this leg?'

'Why not? You still have to eat.'

'It doesn't look very elegant, that's all. Do you really want to be seen with a limping woman on your arm?'

'People's opinions of me are their reality, not mine.'

'I've not got any suitable clothes.'

'We can take care of that. Any other excuses?'

She laughed. 'You really want to go out to dinner?'

'Yes, I do!'

Simon arranged for a personal dresser from Stella McCartney's SoHo boutique to bring a collection of clothing to the penthouse.

'I can't wear these,' Soraya whispered. 'They're way out of my league. You've seen how I dress.'

'Yes, but you're not in Rainbow Valley now. You're in New York city, and you're my guest.'

Soraya chose half a dozen dresses, and matching shoes; guilt marring any pleasure she felt.

'Simon, it's ridiculous wearing clothes which cost this much. It's wasted on me with this leg.'

'I'll decide if that's the case.'

When he smiled, she was right back to that first morning when he walked in the door of House of Hearts. One day she'd confess that she knew who he was the second she laid eyes on him. That million-dollar smile was instantly recognisable. Yes, she'd confess that he was the reason she spoke so quickly and fumbled about like an idiot. And she'd have to confide in him that he had made her into the astute business woman she was. And when she confessed, she'd admit that she'd been watching his financial reports since she was 19 years old. It was the day she decided not to be a Cinderella, but to be responsible for her own income. Not today though. Being Cinderella off to the ball might actually be fun. Today she was more than willing to be a princess of sorts.

'I can dress myself,' she insisted. When she hobbled out, on crutches, half an hour later, Simon stared.

The black-flower macramé one-shoulder dress featured all-over lace with a nude lining. It completely covered her leg. Though her crutches were more than visible, Simon didn't see them. No, he was transfixed by the vision before him. Was this really the Pollyanna girl who lived in floral skirts and socks?

'I told you it wouldn't work!' she snapped when he didn't say anything.

'Oh it works, Soraya. It works. You look absolutely stunning.'

'So why did it take you so long to say anything? That was the longest minute of my life!'

'My approval means that much to you?'

'Let's go!' she said, frowning. This was probably not the time to tell him how darned dashing he looked in his Brioni tuxedo. And did he have to smell so good?

For the first time since she fell down the stairs, she was grateful for her plastered leg. The sheer weight of it meant she was unlikely to fall over every time she breathed him in. Soraya found that he was utterly intoxicating, not only to look at, but to stand near. More than once she closed her eyes to deliberately block him out while she regained her composure, but she quickly learnt that it was impossible. Everything about him permeated the room; his presence was imposing, but in a non-threatening way.

'This is Delmonico's. It was built in 1837. Many presidents have dined here.'

Soraya marvelled at the elegant setting, and as she looked through the menu, it was clear that culinary creativity was what gave it its name. A bouquet of sweetly scented stargazer lilies and white freesias was delivered to their table, with a card inside. Soraya opened it to read: *Welcome to New York!*

'I hope you take away fond memories of the city,' Simon said, reaching for her hand. 'I want you to enjoy yourself.'

'Thank you,' she said softly, blushing a little. How could she not enjoy herself when she had him to look at every day? Everything about Simon Beaudin was the stuff of romance novels: the classic male. A perfect physique. A dashing smile. Truth was, she couldn't have dreamed him up if she tried. They chatted idly for a while, once again coming back to the subject of money. Simon asked her about investments and savings.

Soraya stopped him short. 'One of the reasons we call money currency is because it needs to flow, as in the word *current*. As soon as you start focusing on hoarding, then it stops the flow. Circulation is vital to a healthy financial life, whether you're giving it away to a good cause, paying bills or sharing it. You're either circulating money or congesting it.'

'That's all very well, Soraya, but even you put money away for a rainy day.'

'Yes, but I ensure that plenty of it is circulating first.' Soraya was about to start on another point of view when something wholly unexpected caught her eye. No, it couldn't be? It was! The President and the First Lady were being shown to the table closest to them. There were six tables in the room, and they were seated next to the President of the United States?

Soraya was sure she was dreaming. This was *all* a dream. Soon she'd wake up, and be sewing love hearts in her shop.

They shared two entrées: acquerello risotto; Chiogga beets, pumpkin, roasted fennel and parmesan, followed by Chanterelles and parsnip in aged maple.

Throughout dinner Soraya quizzed him about his past: where he went to school, parents, siblings, cousins, girlfriends, education. The more questions she asked, the less chance there was of him asking about her life; which was just how she liked it. The last thing she needed was him getting under her skin more than he already had.

'I told you, I can't keep eating desserts like this,' she protested, tucking into the red-apple cheesecake: pecan crunch, apple glaze, and Bourbon cranberry ice cream.

'You can use my gym,' he offered. 'There are plenty of ways you can burn off the calories that don't involve that left leg of yours.'

Although she wasn't entirely sure if he intended to deliver that last line with a double meaning, her face registered the possibility, and his smile indicated that he noticed exactly where her thoughts were heading.

Soraya was oblivious to the couple entering the dining room. Simon looked up and acknowledged the familiar face of the Formula 1 driver, while Soraya finished her dessert.

'Soraya? Soraya Juniper? Is that *you*? I barely recognised you! How long has it been?'

If there was anything she could erase about New York, it was this exact moment.

'Seven years. Seven years in December. December 24th.' Nothing else needed to be said. They both remembered the day. It would be forever etched into their consciousness. Christmas was never the same again. How could it be?

'You're looking fantastic. Amazing. I've never seen you dressed like…well, you look incredible. This is my wife, Anna. Anna, this is Soraya.'

'I've heard a lot about you,' Anna said, her smile conveying a sense of pity and sadness.

Simon didn't miss a trick. There was history here, and it was obvious that Soraya didn't want it spread across the dining table as if it was just another meal to linger over.

'This is Simon Beaudin.'

'Hi Simon. Recognised you straight away. We've followed a lot of your advice over the years. Lovely to be able to thank you personally for that.'

'You're welcome. Are you dining here for a special occasion?' Simon asked.

'Our wedding anniversary. Three years.'

Simon caught the ghostly look on Soraya's face.

'Don't let us hold you up. Enjoy your evening, and congratulations!' Simon said.

'Shall we go?' he asked Soraya, his voice was soft and concerned as he reached his hand out to hold hers.

'Yes. I had a lovely evening, Simon. Thank you.'

'My pleasure.'

# Secrets Revealed

Simon helped Soraya into bed, adjusting the pillow until she was comfortable, then paused for a moment, tucking a wisp of hair behind her ear. Their eyes caught, as they often did, and they allowed themselves to linger in that space that was both safe and comfortable, and yet fraught with danger and a future neither of them could see. Desperate to ask about December 24th, and what connected her to the hottest name in Formula 1, he resisted. It had to come from her. Simon wasn't sure how patient he could be, though. As she drifted off to sleep, he headed to his studio to write.

*This book is never going to get finished if I keep working on the novel,* he chided himself. But tonight it didn't matter. Writing allowed him to channel the angst he was feeling. The thought that Soraya was keeping something from him became unbearable. Not that it was his business, but he felt they were developing a friendship and he wanted her to feel safe enough to share.

Three hours later, he decided to turn in for the night. It was just the softest sound, but he heard it before he opened the bedroom door. Was she crying?

'Soraya, are you okay? You're crying,' he whispered as he entered the dark room. 'Are you in pain? Is there anything I can do?'

'I'm fine, Simon,' she said, wiping the tears from her cheeks.

But she wasn't fine, and he knew it. Simon undressed, and crawled in beside her. Instead of asking any more questions, he simply wrapped his arms around her. At first it seemed as if her rapidly beating heart would explode, but after a few minutes it settled down to a more comfortable pace. Simon kissed her shoulder, and held his hand gently to her cheek.

'You're safe here, Soraya. I'm not going to hurt you. I promise. I hope you can believe that.'

She didn't reply. Liam hadn't intended to hurt her either, and look how that turned out. The scars were still there; scabs ready to be picked off at a moment's notice.

Neither of them slept very well that night, and by six am they were both keen to be out of bed.

'Let me help you shower,' he said.

The double-headed shower was the ultimate in luxury, and Soraya was so taken with it that she almost forgot that he was standing naked beside her. *Almost*.

'I love it when you wash my hair, and the way your fingers deeply massage my scalp. It feels heavenly,' she confessed.

'Soraya, what happened on December 24th, seven years ago?'

There was a long silence. Simon had just about given up expecting her to answer, when her voice cracked and she said 'I buried the love of my life.'

'Oh Soraya,' he said softly, and then held her. Any thought he had of attempting to kiss her this morning disappeared out the air vent with the steam from the shower. For a few moments she wept, then regained her composure. 'I'm so sorry. You don't need me falling apart on you!'

'The grief is obviously still raw. If you need to fall apart, then do. I'm not going to judge you for it.'

'It's been seven years! At some point this has to feel better. I thought I was doing so well, but seeing Ralph last night was like time travelling. I was nineteen years old again and so lost in the world. All my dreams and the life we were planning just went. Bang. Crash. And he was gone!' This time she wailed into Simon's strong chest, unashamedly letting out years of repressed pain.

'The night before he died, Liam proposed. I said I'd tell him the answer the next day. I wanted to say yes straight away, but I wanted him to focus on the big day he had coming up.'

'What happened?'

'He was killed in a racing-car accident. Mercifully, he died instantly, but the image of his crumpled body has never left me. I'm haunted by the fact he never knew that I always planned to say yes. I don't understand why I didn't just say yes straight away,' she said, feeling Simon squeeze her just that bit tighter. Just enough to let her know that he was there, holding her, caring about her, and ready to be the shoulder she needed to cry on.

'Have you had any relationships since then?'

'Isn't that enough drama for one lifetime?'

'I was only asking. Please don't be cross at me Soraya. I care about you. I don't like to see you hurting.'

After breakfast, Simon said he wanted to write for a few hours, and then he'd take her out to lunch.

Soraya sat at the dining table with her laptop on, waited until he left the room, and then began to look through her files.

The morning's conversation about Liam had triggered something deep and wounding, and she needed to channel the energy. After two hours of non-stop typing, she decided to sit on the sofa for a few minutes and shut her eyes. She was so tired. Deep emotion was exhausting. Soraya looked forward to the cast being removed so she could sleep properly again.

*Just a few minutes*, she promised herself, as she closed her eyes.


Simon entered the dining area just before noon. Soraya's gentle snores made him smile. Curiosity got the better of him, and he glanced at the computer screen. Was she a Facebook girl or a Twitter one?

When he saw the words *Ashley Starr*, followed by Soraya's address: *House of Hearts, Main Street, Rainbow Valley* at the top of the Word document, he tried to make sense of it.

Ashley Starr? But that's the romance novelist, he thought to himself. Is she stalking her? He looked at the snoring angel on the sofa, and the penny dropped. *Jesus!* Soraya was living a double life: shopkeeper by day, novelist by night. No wonder she only worked a four-hour day!

Simon headed back to his study and googled Ashley Starr.

Ashley Starr: award-winning romance novelist, on the USA Today bestseller list no less than twenty times. She began writing at 19 years of age.

It didn't take a mathematical genius to work out that it was around the same time as Liam had been killed. Why had she kept her writing a secret?


'Fancy a little workout in the gym before we have lunch?'

'You're joking, right?'

'Not at all. Come on.'

Simon led her to a room off from the library. It was

an elite fitness studio with state-of-the art equipment. 'I don't have time to travel to a gym each day. This makes my life a bit easier. Here, you can come and do some gentle arm weights. Like this,' he said, demonstrating some free weights. 'Weight resistance usually burns more calories than cardio so don't be too bothered about not exercising that leg.'

Simon watched her do several repetitions, and then said, 'Try this. It's a fly machine, and it's great. You can do so many different exercises.'

'I'm going to leave New York with toned arms!'

'They look pretty toned to me already,' he smiled, touching her elbow gently.

'This is quite fun, actually,' she laughed. 'Never thought of myself as a gym girl before, but I like how strong this makes me feel.'

'That's probably more important than ever. It's easy to feel like a victim when your leg's broken.'

'Have you ever broken your leg?' she asked.

'Twice! I grew up on a horse stud; got bucked off a stallion and broke both legs at once. I know the importance of having someone help you get clean,' he laughed. 'Not that I appreciated that when I was a fifteen-year-old pubescent boy and my mother was bathing me! And don't even start me on toilets!'

'Oh dear!' she laughed, grateful for the lightness of their conversation.

'Showering with you is an altogether different experience,' Simon said, his eyes lingering on her face long enough for Soraya to turn away.

'I hope that's a good thing,' she murmured.

'Have you heard me complaining?' he chuckled.

'I'm sure you will after doing this each day for several weeks!'

'I doubt it!'

They used several pieces of equipment, with Soraya feeling more and more at home in the gym.

On the rear deltoid machine, she worked on strengthening her back muscles. Soraya could feel Simon standing right behind her, and closed her eyes to breathe in the scent of his aftershave. It was intoxicating! When she stopped for a moment to catch her breath, she felt his hands come down on her shoulders.

'Are you okay?' he asked.

'Couldn't be better,' she lied. Right at this moment she felt out of control. All she wanted to do was feel his naked body against hers. That wasn't too much to ask, surely? She reached up and placed her hand over one of his. The connection between them was like lightning, and she felt her pulse quicken. The man was driving her crazy. Making love was inevitable, she knew that. What she didn't know was when it was going to happen. Soraya found herself feeling incredibly impatient. What were they waiting for?

'That's probably enough exercise for you for one day,' Simon said, removing his hands from her shoulders. 'Come on, let's go.'

Soraya hoped her happy mood would carry on through the afternoon. It was such a stark contrast to the night before.

Simon helped her dress in a fluid tunic in soft-linen tone with a sheer lower skirt loosely attached with slashes through the seam. Simon stood back to admire her in the feminine, floaty silhouette that the dress created.

'You really look fantastic.'

'A bit overdressed for lunch, though, don't you think?'

'Not at all!' he smiled, passing the crutches. 'Not at all.'

They took the lift to the ground floor, and Simon helped her into the back of a limousine.

'We're not catching a bus then?' she laughed.

'Not today, princess.' Their eyes caught, and their smiles were evidence that there'd been a huge shift in their relationship. Simon was courting her, and she finally realised that. But why? she wondered. They were from different worlds. Him, a city boy in finance. Her, a country girl in romance. They were so wrong for each other. Why was he even bothering?

They arrived at Club 21, and proceeded to the bar. Simon ordered an artisan beer for himself, and a white wine for Soraya. She felt a little dizzy, not because she was unwell, but because she could easily count at least half a dozen famous faces in the room. So this is where the famous hang out, she thought to herself. Simon had secured them a cosy sofa by the wood-burning fire.

'Afterwards we can go the Museum of Modern Art or take in a show at Broadway,' Simon said, while looking through the menu.

'Or both?' she smiled. That caught his attention. There was something about her smile that completely dazzled him. Simon was grateful to be sitting down, because he sure as hell would have lost his balance otherwise.

'Yes, most definitely both!' Then he studied her hair, and face, and let his eyes linger at her breast line.

'You don't look like a woman who went tumbling down the stairs a few days ago.'

'At this moment, I don't feel like it, either. Thank you Simon.'

'My pleasure.'

Soraya was just about to start eating her entrée: a Portobello tower with Bloomsdale spinach, Autumn-squash ratatouille, beet and olive quinoa-stuffed piquillo pepper, when Simon said, 'Would you ever have told me that you're Ashley Starr?'

And with just those two words, her fork dropped, and her mouth opened.

'How the hell...'

'Your laptop was open when you fell asleep. I saw it at the top of the document.'

'I have reasons for protecting my privacy, and I'd like to keep that part of my life firmly behind closed doors!' she hissed, making it clear that he was on dangerous ground and should back off.

'I'm not trying to pry, just curious. Off the record, is your writing career funding House of Hearts?'

'No! *Absolutely not*. It is self sufficient, and thriving. I can't believe you'd even ask that!'

Simon studied her body language. There was nothing to indicate that she was lying; she was just mad as hell. *Mad at him!* When he didn't say anything else, she continued speaking.

'You can go through all my accounts if you don't believe me. Look, I love being a romance novelist. It might seem light and fluffy and inconsequential to someone like you, but I enjoy it. There's so much fun to be had creating a world with characters that are destined to meet and live happily ever after. I get as much pleasure from writing as my devoted fans get from reading. But writing—*this* sort of writing—is an isolating experience. I live alone. I work alone. I have the shop so I can mix with people! There are so many times I've derived inspiration from eavesdropping on my customers. I need to be part of life in order to write about it. Can you understand that?'

'Completely. I just wish you had told me.'

'It wasn't any of your business, Simon. Besides, what difference does it make? You were interviewing me about House of Hearts, not about Ashley Starr.'

'It just feels like such a huge thing to not share.'

'If it makes you feel any better, my best friend doesn't even know. My editor, Santana and my parents are the only people who know that I write novels.'

'And me.'

'Yes, Simon, and you. Let's keep it that way.' Acutely aware that her secret identity hung in the balance, she frowned at the knowledge that Simon held it in his hands, and the possibilities terrified her.


Simon fiddled with his meal: sautéed sole, asparagus, lemon-butter sauce. Why had he lost his appetite? Something was disturbing him, and he wasn't sure why. Shouldn't he be pleased that she was so successful? As she said, it made no difference to the income of House of Hearts. It didn't affect his writing about the shop.

'No dessert for me,' Soraya insisted when the waiter came by.

'We'll share. Two forks, please,' Simon instructed him.

'Simon? I said…'

'You're worried about putting on weight, I know. Let's share. It's always nice to finish with something sweet.'

The truth was that he hoped it would soften her, and sweeten her mood.

The Grand Marnier soufflé and crème Chantilly with medley of berries defied words. Simon listened as she moaned discreetly at the sensations in her mouth. 'This is amazing.'

'Glad you had some, then?'

'Are you always right?'

'Yes,' he said, reaching for her hand, 'except when I'm wrong.'

Both of their smiles widened. They were grateful that they couldn't read each other's mind, though they suspected that the images going through them were the same.

'May I ask how you got into writing romance novels?' The last thing he wanted to do was scare her off again with probing questions, but he also didn't want her slipping back to Rainbow Valley without knowing everything there was to possibly know about her.

'When Liam was killed, I had just started working at the local fabric shop. I had no great ambition in life. When he died, I hid myself away in my parents' house and retreated from the world. I received so many packets, parcels and boxes of goodwill from people. Trinkets, cards, homemade meals. It was such an outpouring of love but I was numb to it all. I just couldn't see a life ahead of me. In one of the care packets was a romance novel. I was so angry. I mean, how dare my cousin send me a happily-ever-after when my world was just torn apart? How thoughtless! I threw it in the bin. I was fuming. At three in the morning, when I couldn't sleep, I retrieved it and started reading. I sat up for two hours until I'd finished, then slept like a baby. I can't describe it, but something about the ending filled me with peace.'

'Even though your life was at complete odds with that?'

'It gave me hope, I suppose. Maybe it wasn't my destiny to have love long term, but perhaps I could help other people find their soul mate?'

'So you started writing?'

'Not straight away. I did start devouring romance novels, though. I mostly stayed in my parents' house and started making crafts by day. Hearts. That's all I could make,' she laughed. 'At night, I read. One day I saw an advert for a So You Want To Be A Writer competition. I don't know what possessed me to think I could possibly write a novel, but I submitted a few chapters. Turned out to be quite therapeutic, actually. I was in such a state of grief, and putting that into words was a life-saving act.'

'And then what happened?'

'My room was overloaded with hearts is what happened. It had become a bit of an obsession. Mum said 'If you're going to keep making all these hearts, would you at least sell them?' And so I started with a stall at the market. Two months later, I took out the lease on the building that is now House of Hearts.'

'Wow, that quickly?'

'Yeah. The house was really run down, so the landlord gave me six months' grace while I painted it and did some interior-design work. I won the competition, which was incredibly amazing, but I was immediately offered a five-book contract. It changed my life.'

'And yet you keep it a secret?'

'It's not a secret to me, and that's all that matters. I don't think my readers care.'

'Do you have fears around people judging you for your wealth?'

'No, not at all. I'd love to be a role model for other women about the brilliance of being financially self-sufficient. So many of them have a hidden fear of supporting themselves. It's called the Cinderella Complex. We grow up dreaming of Prince Charming coming along to rescue us. Life isn't quite like that. Women sabotage themselves every time they ignore their inner potential.'

'You can see the irony, though, can't you? You write 'boy meets girl' and he's bound to be rich? Aren't you encouraging them to be Cinderella?'

'I'm writing to a genre framework. Trust me, my heroines are feisty enough not to be Cinderella!'

Simon laughed out loud. 'Why doesn't that surprise me?'

'I've had wealthy heroines in some of my non-series novels.'

'So, can I ask you about investments? Where do you put your money? I'm asking as a professional, not as your date.'

Soraya wasn't sure if this was the time, but it was going to have to come out at some point, it may as well be now. And besides, what could be worse than him knowing her secret identity?

'When you arrived at House of Hearts, I knew exactly who you were. I've been watching you on Good Morning since I was nineteen. I had so much money for the first time in my life, and I panicked a bit. I went to Dennis Dyson, the bank manager, for investment advice. Remember him? You met him that morning. It was his suggestion that I start following you both on TV and in the print media. Told me I couldn't go wrong.'

Simon laughed. 'Really?'

'Honestly.'

Soraya shifted in her seat and tried wiggling the toes of her left leg. Ouch, it *still* hurt to do that.

'So you bought the land behind your home from your book royalties rather than House of Hearts income?'

'Yes. I was also able to buy the building a couple of years later. When my books made it onto the USA Today Bestseller lists, my income shot through the roof. I helped Santana set up her florist. I invested in a building, delivery vehicles, and provided a year's worth of income so she could hire staff.'

'Stocks? Bonds? Offshore investments? Where else have you put your money?'

'Scholarships for underprivileged teens to get them into creative writing, and I fund an orphanage in Kenya. I have a few apartments in Boston that I lease out to a legal firm.'

'You like investing in property then?'

'It always seems like a sound thing to do. People need places to live and work from. That's what you said once, and I wrote it into my diary! I've learnt from the best,' she smiled, and spontaneously reached for his hand; a gesture which surprised them both given how reserved she'd been about any physical contact. 'Thank you, Simon. I owe you a lot.'

'You know, I feel at a disadvantage here. You seem to know a lot about me.'

'And you, me. I think we're even.'

'No, we're not. I feel like I've barely scratched the surface. I want to know more. Soraya, I want to know everything about you. I'm not talking professionally, but personally.'

'Simon, you said nothing would happen...'

'Unless you wanted it to.'

'Please don't say that.'

'Why?'

'Two words: chalk and cheese. We're not suited to each other. Opposites might attract, but they also repel. I would like to walk away from here with a friendship. I'd really like that. Anything else is asking for trouble.'

'So we both agree that there's an attraction?'

He was playing with her!

'You know as well as I do that there is! A blind man could see what's going on.'

'And you're not willing to enjoy that, and see where it takes us?'

'It's not going to take us anywhere. You know that. Why are you even asking?'

'Because, Soraya, I like you very much and I'd like to get to know you better,' he whispered so the other diners wouldn't overhear.

'That may be how it works in your world, but not in mine. Simon, I don't do flings. That's not how I'm wired. I'm an 'all or nothing' girl, and frankly, I don't want 'all' with anyone. I'm happy on my own.'

'So that's the end of it then?'

'Yes.' She placed her fork down. 'I'm sorry.'

'Would Liam want that for you?' The words were out before he even had a chance to consider the impact that they'd have.

'Don't bring him into this relationship! There's no comparison between...'

Soraya stood up, reached for her crutches, and said 'I want to go.'

'No. We're going to finish this conversation, no matter how difficult it is for you. Sit down, and answer my question because whether you like it or not, he *is* part of this relationship.' His voice was gentle but firm.

'Who the hell do you think you are?' She was barely muttering the words, but he heard them loud and clear.

'I'm someone who has grown to care for you, and I see you living in a jail of old memories. It's time to move on.'

'I'll decide if and when I move on, thank you very much. I can't believe what you're actually saying to me! You're so insensitive.'

'No, I'm not being insensitive. I'm being honest. Death is horrible. Losing someone the way you did, at the threshold of adult life, when you had so many dreams ahead of you, was absolutely shocking. It still is. But you're one of the most incredible women I've ever met, and the thought of you hiding yourself from the world, and from a man loving you, is just crazy.'

'So I'm crazy now?'

'Frankly, yes.'

'There are two certainties: you can't buy love, and you can't hold onto it. Love hurts. I have no desire to go back there again. I've said it now, are you happy?'

'No, sweetheart,' he said, reaching for her hand and kissing it. 'Love doesn't hurt. Rejection hurts. Loss crucifies you. Jealousy can rip you to shreds. Loneliness erodes the soul. These aren't love though, so don't confuse them.'

'And you're an expert on love?' she mocked.

'I know as much about love as the next man or woman. You can't use previous relationships to determine how future ones may pan out. It's pointless.

It's like blaming a used-car salesman for all the dodgy cars you've had, even though he didn't sell them to you. At some point, you have to take responsibility for your feelings, and own them.'

She stood up again, and glared at him. 'I want to go now.'

'Museum, then? Or Broadway?'

'Home. My home.'

'That's not happening. I promised your sister.'

'You can't keep me hostage here!'

Simon passed her his cell phone. 'Be my guest. Tell her you want to go home because I spoke a few home truths.'

'How dare you! I want to go home. I'll catch a bus if I have to. I've had enough, Simon.'

'Okay, if that's what you want. Let's go.' Simon motioned to the waiter, and then stood up to help her with the crutches. What neither of them had counted on was the effect his cologne was about to have on her.

Soraya tried to ignore the conservative masculine fragrance composed of spice, wood and vanilla notes. The top notes, intensive and fresh, including rosewood and coriander, gave way to the warmer and mysterious Bulgarian rose, carnation and warm cinnamon, and then into a lingering base composed of sandalwood, intensive vanilla and ambrette seeds. It was a heady combination, which ignited her deepest primal urges and left her floundering for any sense of control and logical thinking.

'What are you wearing?' she hissed.

'Sorry?'

'Why do you have to smell so good?'

Simon moved in a little closer, a smile changing the entire look on his face. 'And you want to walk away from that?' Simon knew better than to laugh, but he couldn't hide his amusement at how vulnerable she was when he stood this close to her.

'I *have* to walk away from that. I need to think straight. Let me grab my bag, and then you can take me to the bus station.'

'Soraya...'

'No, Simon. Don't say anything. I don't want to hear anything that you have to say.'

'It's Chanel Egoïste Original.'

'Oh.'

'You can wait here in the limousine, if you like, while I pack your bags.'

'No, I'll come with you and make sure I have everything.'

'You don't trust me?'

'I didn't say that. I just would feel better seeing for myself that everything is packed.'

It was a stony-silent few minutes as they left the limo and ascended to the penthouse suite.

Soraya placed her laptop into its case, and left it on the table with an overnight bag containing stationery. Just as she was collecting paperwork, strong hands came up behind her and wrapped around her waist.

'I'm sorry.' His voice was genuinely apologetic, and when she didn't resist, Simon kissed her softly on the side of her neck. 'I am truly sorry. Please don't go. I really would like you to stay.'

If the cologne almost worked in the restaurant, it sure as hell was going to work here: in private.

Simon could feel his arousal pressing against her, and made no attempt to disguise his feelings.

'It's just lust, Simon. Don't read anything more into what's happening. You can have any woman you want, don't chase me. You're wasting your time.'

'Am I?'

Soraya felt his breath heavy against her skin. He smelt so darn good. Simon kissed her again, and she felt his cheek against the inner slope of her neck. There was comfort in his touch, and she fought in vain to bring herself back to reality.

'What are you doing, Simon? Come on, let's go now.'

'No. Now I'm going to be the stubborn one. I know you want me as much as I want you. Enough with the resistance.'

'Simon!'

This time, he turned her around. Slowly. It wasn't quite a pirouette, but it felt like a beautiful movement from a sensuous ballet. The tenderness it evoked in both of them caught Soraya and Simon quite by surprise. In that moment of time standing still, she slipped into his deep blue eyes.

'What is so wrong with me wanting to make love to you?'

'Because you wouldn't be, you'd just be having sex. There's a difference!'

'When we become naked and open ourselves to each other, it won't just be sex, Soraya. I promise you. We're not animals, we're human.'

Simon's hands reached behind her head, bringing her face closer to him, and then his lips met hers. From the moment he set eyes on her, that fateful morning in the House of Hearts, he'd wanted to do this. Her lips tasted of the dessert she'd eaten, and he found the hint of Grand Marnier rather erotic as his tongue searched her mouth for a hint that she would say yes. Was it wrong to want to make love to Soraya?

Simon was not about to ask her. He couldn't bear the thought that this moment might end. Instead, he lifted her up into his arms and carried her to his bed.

'You're a good kisser,' she whispered, working hard to keep a poker face.

'Only because the subject makes it easy.' Simon studied her for a moment, and then undressed. When her eyes dipped away, he said 'It's okay, I don't mind if you watch.'

Soraya had seen his body before, in the shower, but this was different. That body was going to become one with her. No longer was he in caretaker mode; Simon was about to become her lover.

'You can't make love with a broken leg.'

'I'm making love with you, not your leg. Let me worry about the technicalities. I'm a smart man, I'll figure it out.' He smiled, then leaned forward and, touching her cheek, said 'You're so gorgeous, even when you're angry.'

Soraya reached for his chest, her hand marking out each ripped muscle: lean, taut, powerful. Then she pressed her palm into him as if she was tattooing herself permanently into his heart area.

As he unzipped his trousers, Simon felt Soraya watch his long, toned legs as he stepped out of them. His silk boxers slid off with ease.

All she could think was: *he sunbathes naked.*

It was obvious from his lean muscles that he not only worked out in his gym, but ate a balanced diet, not one rich with desserts. He'd clearly wanted to spoil her while she was in the city.

An involuntary moan betrayed her. Sure, she wrote about handsome, breathtaking physiques for a living, and was quite capable of making her pulse race with the literary prowess of her imagination as it took flight, but this? This man left her breathless.

'Simon? Be gentle,' she said, as her hand reached for his arm, holding it as if to reiterate her message.

For the new few minutes, Simon sat on the side of the bed, slowly undressing Soraya, and stopping to kiss her from time to time. She didn't need to say so, but he could feel her body responding in anticipation of where they were heading.

'I have an idea,' he said, scooping her up, and carrying her naked body into the lounge.

'Where are we going?'

'Somewhere a little more comfortable for our purposes.'

The late afternoon Sun shone through the floor-to-ceiling windows, adding a natural warmth and golden ambience to the room. 'Don't worry, no one will see you.'

Simon made himself comfortable on the slipper chair—an armless upholstered chair with short legs—then encouraged her to sit on him. Her leg wasn't plastered all the way up, so she was able to bend at the knee slightly. Simon held her narrow naked waist, so she didn't need to put so much pressure on her knee, and pulled her closer to him.

'You've really thought this out, haven't you?' she smiled.

'I've had a few days to think about it,' he admitted.

Soraya had to laugh. Had he really been planning

to make love to her from the day they met? If she was honest, she'd been having those very same thoughts. Was it any surprise that they were here together, right now, like this?

His hands expertly soothed all the tension from her back, and he leaned forward to feel the softness of her breasts against his cheeks.

'Mmmm,' he moaned. 'You feel so good.'

'You need to shave!' she said. 'That's ticklish.'

'Hmm, do you like being tickled?'

'No!'

His lips teased her nipples, until she couldn't bear it any more.

'Just kiss me!'

'So you're finally admitting that chalk and cheese can get along then?'

She loved how he always managed to make her laugh. His kiss was lingering, and deliberate, and Soraya felt sensations that she didn't know were possible in the human body. Like a tribal war beat, the drumming grew incessantly louder.

'You like that then?' he said, his fingers gently working their magic: teasing, taming, tightening.

All she could do was moan gently in acknowledgement. She was surprised how unselfconscious she was, sitting here in his home, completely naked in broad daylight. No, not sitting. Straddling. Straddling wide, and her hair hanging wildly over her shoulders, flicking with each moan and movement of her head.

'And do you like this?' he chuckled, watching her head tilt in the opposite direction.

Words had long gone; her sighs would have to suffice. Of course she liked it! Her mouth had no way of telling him that, other than to open as her head swung back in ecstasy, and her eyelids closed.

Every deft touch, the way his natural body odour smelled of the earthy spice cumin, his warm breath against her neck: all had a way of making her lose control. This was so far away from her day-to-day reality that she convinced herself it was a dream. She couldn't possibly be making love with Simon Beaudin.

But as she felt his hands move down, down, down, over and firmly onto her hips, pulling her forward, she knew this wasn't a dream. Everything was real. *He* was real. His chest felt firm and powerful against her ample malleable breasts. Chalk and cheese. Firm and soft. Yang and yin. An intense throbbing pulsation deep in her core told Soraya one thing: she wanted him inside her. And she wasn't prepared to wait any longer.

Simon, however, had other ideas. This was an afternoon that he didn't want to end. As far as he was concerned, the day had only just begun. It felt like an eternity had passed since the moment he first laid eyes on her, and became aware of the first stirrings of healthy male sexuality warning him that destiny was knocking. If he entered her now, they'd be that much closer to getting to the end, and he wasn't ready for that. Not yet. Not now.

Every movement that Soraya made to get closer to him, to become one with him, was thwarted by Simon kissing another part of her body. If she hadn't had a broken leg, she'd have simply positioned herself exactly where she wanted—*needed*—to be.

So close, and yet so far! Was he trying to drive her crazy? Trying to get her to…*beg*?

Simon became acutely aware that he was driving her to distraction, and that she was reliant on him to change position. He gently lowered his hand down further, finally reaching the hot apex at the crest of her legs.

'Oh,' she moaned, tossing her hair back over her shoulders. 'Oooooh. You look happy,' she said, aware of his mischief making.

'You're trembling,' he replied, his groan of satisfaction causing them both to close their eyes for a moment. He forced his eyes open, and then gently cupped her chin. 'Look at me, Soraya.'

Simon then firmly held both of her wrists to stop her from trying to bring them closer, and kissed her rosy nipple. He wanted to bring time to a standstill.

Spirals of ecstasy threatened her ability to stay in control. Whatever he was doing, whatever game he was playing to slow things down, had the desired effect on both of them: it accelerated the heat between them. Every minute movement, scent, touch and sound became a symphony of pleasure.

'Open your eyes,' he asked. 'I want to see you. I want to see the look in your eyes when I do this.'

Soraya slowly opened her lazy lids, and tried to regain focus, then as his hand elicited the dampness her body was yielding, her eyes widened. A shudder rippled from her centre.

'Simon,' she whispered, 'I'm ready.'

'Really?' he laughed. 'Are you sure?'

'Come on. I can't wait…I need you.'

'I want to be sure you want this as much as I do, because once we start, there's no going back.'

'I do.' As those words came out, so sure, so certain, she imagined them being used in another context, and how she never got to say them to Liam. In a split second she went from unbridled ecstasy to feeling as if she was cheating on Liam.

'What's wrong?' Simon asked, detecting the shadow slip across her face.

Soraya shook her head as if to say 'nothing's wrong', but within two seconds Simon had lifted her up, and widened her straddle to accommodate him. *All of him.*

'Oh,' she moaned, as he entered her.

'Is that what you were waiting for?' he chuckled, slowly easing himself inside her until they finally fitted together. *Perfection!*

With a gentle thrust, he found his way further inside her, exploring, searching, and savouring the intense pulsations throbbing between them.

'Yes, I want that, but…'

'I forgot. Condoms are in the bedroom.'

'Seriously? You expect me to run and get them with this leg?' she laughed.

'No, I don't. Soraya, don't move. Stay right where you are.'

Simon somehow managed to lift her up with him as he stood up and gained his footing. The change in position intensified his place inside her.

'Simon,' she gasped.

Then he pulled her down further onto him, tighter, pushing himself into her as far as he could go.

'Hold tight,' he said, walking them both to the bedroom, and praying that he wouldn't climax early. He fought every urge to let go and surrender to the torrent of sensations rapidly building up inside him. She felt so damn good!

'Don't break your back,' she warned.

'I'm hardly going to do that, not when we've come this far,' he promised, hoping he wouldn't come at all. At least, not yet. Not until they'd had some time to play. Time to get to know each other better. Using every last inch of restraint, he moaned each time she clenched firmly against him. The woman was a tormenter!

As he bent forward into a drawer to retrieve an unopened packet, she sighed.

Simon kissed her neck, and for a few moments they just stood there, searching each other's eyes. At some point they'd have to come apart so he could put the condom on. *At some point.* Not now. Not when everything about their union felt so thrilling.

The most startling thought occurred to Simon: what would happen if they didn't use a condom? What was he protecting her from? He had no sexually transmitted diseases. Pregnancy? Surely she'd make a great mother. He mentally shook his head. Don't be stupid! There is only today. There will *not* be a future with Soraya Juniper. Chalk and cheese. She said so herself. We've only got today. He hoped like hell she couldn't read his thoughts.

'Are you okay?' Soraya asked.

'Perfectly,' he smiled. 'Now, where were we?'

As Simon made them both comfortable again on the slipper chair, he lifted her off and onto his firm thighs.

'Here, let me,' she offered, taking the packet from his hand.

If he wasn't aroused before, what she was about to do to him would change everything. To the tinker of crunching foil, Soraya kissed him. Tiny kisses perched across his chest, his dark hair a gentle cushion as she kissed his strong pectoral muscles. Her hands took charge, and without even needing to look at what she was doing, a practical task became one of the most erotically charged moments of Simon's life. For a woman with next to no experience with men, she covered the head and length of him without batting an eyelid or losing eye contact with him. He couldn't even do that without studiously examining himself.

'Thank you,' he murmured.

'The pleasure is all mine,' Soraya said, her body increasingly tormented by the break in procedures.

'Are you ready?' he asked, and at the nod of her head, Simon lifted her onto him.

They moaned in unison, both wondering how long they were going to last. The past few moments hadn't deterred them, but magnified the intensity of their longing.

With each thrust, Soraya called out; her ecstasy turned him on. *He* was having this effect on her. It was *his* body, and their connection, that was causing her to cry out in ways that women never showed in public. Simon found it hard to reconcile that the sweet woman from House of Hearts, who spent her days sewing fabric lavender bags, was not only a deeply desirable woman, but one with an innate sense of her own body: of what she loved, and what she needed.

'I'm sorry we're limited by positions,' she whispered.

'Are you kidding?' Simon groaned. 'This is perfect. I get to see all of you,' he said. 'All of you. Every beautiful inch of you. Soraya, you're gorgeous.'

'You're not bad yourself,' she chuckled, and with that, Simon guided himself deeper and stronger and further until neither of them could contain the dam of sensations any longer.

A flood of release rocked their world to the core. Life would never be the same again. How could it be, when they were catapulted to the stars? They'd crossed a threshold, taking each other to a wholly new place. A new world. One in which they were both strangers, and where they only had each other for company. They exploded together, sated, and sinking into each other until they didn't know where the other stopped and they started.

Afterwards, Simon lifted Soraya over to sofa, and brought a duvet from the bedroom. She lay back in his arms, as the Sun set across the city.

'This is beautiful,' she murmured.

'You're beautiful.'

'This is like a dream,' she said.

They fell asleep for an hour or so, and then woke with smiles on their faces. *It hadn't been a dream.*

The amber light of the New York evening suffused the room.

'Hungry?' Simon asked.

'Starving!'

'Hmmm,' he whispered, nibbling her neck. 'So am I. Are you thinking what I'm thinking?'

The both laughed, and Simon allowed himself the full pleasure of cupping her soft breasts in each hand. It had been a fantastic afternoon, and they looked forward to the long night ahead of them.

# Different Worlds

The next few days found them creating their own rhythm. Soraya and Simon would spend the mornings working on their writing, followed by time in his gym, then lunch in a restaurant, and then lovemaking on the slipper chair. It was as if they were enveloped in a bubble that time forgot, immune from the cares of the world.

Soraya found herself thinking ahead of time, and about when she returned to Rainbow Valley. Without him. Without Simon Beaudin. She didn't like where her thoughts led her, and felt increasingly frustrated that she'd allowed herself to enter into a physical relationship. It was one thing to scratch an itch, it was an entirely different matter to fall for a man.

She had made a vow that she'd never let a man have this impact on her again; and yet, before she knew it, he'd slipped passed her defences.

Soraya felt the low-grade anxiety that had been swirling for the past few days erupt without warning into a panic attack. Her breathing became shallow and rapid, and for a few moments she wondered if she might just pass out. Simon entered the room to refill his coffee.

'Soraya, what's wrong? You look...'

He was immediately at her side.

'I can't breathe. I...'

'Slow down. Hold my hand, look in my eyes. Breathe with me.' He coached her through slow, deep breaths. 'That's better.'

Patiently, he sat by her side for several minutes. 'What happened?'

'*You!* You are what happened. This. Us. We're in

a relationship, and it's terrifying me. I don't know what the future holds, and I feel out of control.'

'Let me tell you a little secret. No one knows what the future holds. All any of us can do is take one day at a time. What is it you want from me? I can't promise you anything, Soraya. You know that.'

'I don't want anything from you, I just...'

Soraya's breathing picked up pace again.

'Slow down. Stop getting ahead of yourself. Let's talk about this without you hyperventilating.'

Simon paced the room, trying to stall time, but he knew that the matter needed addressing. It had been on his mind, too. 'Look, we've been cooped up here too long. I've got an idea. Let me make a phone call, and then let's get out of here.'

'Where are we going?'

'It's a surprise. Pack enough clothes for a few days.'


Two hours later, they were stepping onto Simon's yacht. 'This is Max,' he said, introducing the chef. 'We'll dine alfresco on the deck in a couple of hours.'

'You own this? This is your yacht?' She was breathless. The open bow, and covered sky deck with large windows, highlighted the sights of New York harbour.

'Let me show you around,' Simon offered.

'She's beautiful,' Soraya whispered.

'She is indeed. Everything about her is to do with balance. She's bold and refined; she's elegant and yet combines comfort with performance. *My Darling* was designed and built in Italy with a little Middle Eastern influence.'

'I can see why sea vessels are called *she*. She is so feminine. It's almost like she has a personality of her own, don't you think?'

'Absolutely.' Simon guided her through the deck with its white U-shaped sofa. The armchairs hinted of the Orient.

'The colours are so tasteful,' Soraya said. 'That mix of azure and spring green against the white and beige is so striking. I just never would have expected to see carpet on a yacht.'

'So you like it on here, then?'

'It's so peaceful,' she said, brushing her hand over the elegant mahogany dining table, and eyeing up the dramatic chandelier in the centre.

'Oh my,' she whispered when she entered the luxurious master suite. It had 180-degree panoramic windows with a spacious private deck. The room opened onto a large study, his and hers walk-in wardrobes, and a marble ensuite with hot tub, shower and separate toilets.

'This is stunning,' Soraya said, marvelling at the traditional oriental design. 'It's pure luxury.' She touched the silk curtains, and then ran her hands over gold-leaf decorations. 'A bedroom with a large L-shaped sofa,' she sighed. 'You don't really need the rest of the yacht if you're in this room, do you?'

'No,' he laughed. 'Everything's here. I love coming here to write sometimes. No phone ringing. It's great!'

Soraya made herself comfortable on the plush sofa.

'Don't get too comfortable. I haven't shown you the cinema room yet, and it has the best chairs in there.'

'No, let's stay here for a while,' she smiled. 'It's private.'

Simon sat beside her on the sofa, gently stroking her head.

'Where do you want to go? Cape Cod, Martha's Vineyard, the Mystic Seaport?' he asked.

'Simon, even if we didn't leave the harbour this is amazing. It's like another world.'

'That's the whole idea. You and I need a change of scenery.'

'It doesn't change the situation between us, though, does it?'

'Perhaps not, but why not enjoy each other's company while we can?'

They chatted lightly for some time, stopping occasionally to kiss.

'It must be nearly dinner time,' Simon said. 'Let's go up to the deck.'

Simon turned on the audio system, and sultry saxophone love songs filled the air. 'I know what you're doing, Mr Beaudin.'

'Dance with me,' he said, holding out his hand. 'Come and dance with me.'

The atmosphere on the yacht was elegant and intimate. Soraya would never forget this evening, as she watched the Sun dipping down against the water; the Statue of Liberty silhouetted. As Simon held her close, she allowed herself the luxury of leaning in to him. Why did he always have to feel so good?

'I must be the first woman in history to dance on a luxury yacht with a broken leg.'

'Possibly. You're doing a mighty fine job,' he chuckled. It could hardly be called dancing, when they were barely swaying. The music kept them close, and the aromas from the kitchen found their way up to the open deck.

'I'm famished!' she whispered.

'Are you just?' his voice was husky, raw, almost as if he was unable to keep his feelings under control. 'I want you, Soraya. I want you now.'

'I'm sure the chef would appreciate bringing our dinner up here only to find us enjoying alfresco lovemaking. You should have taken advantage of me while we were in the bedroom!'

'Ah, Max. Yes. Minor detail. He'll be off duty when dinner is over. His lodgings are at the far end of the yacht.'

'He's staying on here with us?'

'Someone has to feed us when we've burned up calories.'

'What exactly are your plans for the next few days?' she asked, but knew the question was pointless.

'To satiate your famished state!'


Max and an assistant arrived with champagne and the chef's specialty: butter-poached Maine lobster with roasted wild mushrooms, gnocchi and cucumber blossoms for Simon; and for Soraya: fresh-water tofu braised with honey-glazed fig, daikon radish and black currant.

'Oh my,' Soraya said, as a linen napkin was unfolded and placed on her lap. Lanterns were lit, and her champagne flute was filled. Bubbles bounced into the air, sending shivers down her spine.

'This is to us,' Simon said, raising his glass. 'May our futures be bright and happy.' At the sound of clinking, Simon continued: 'Let's enjoy whatever the next few days bring us without a concern for the future.'

'If only it were that simple, Simon. Maybe it is for you, but it's not for me.'

'Shhh,' he said softly, holding his hand over hers.

After they'd eaten, Simon invited her to sit on the sofa by the large cast-iron chiminea to keep warm. Soraya looked longingly towards the Jacuzzi. 'What a time to have a broken leg!'

'If you hadn't broken that leg, you wouldn't be here.' As their eyes met, Simon said 'Everything would have been different.'

They made themselves comfortable and sat back in each other's arms, watching the night sky.

'Are you warm enough?' he asked.

'Yes, fine.' Soraya fiddled with the hem of her blouse for a moment, a sign she was nervous. 'Simon, I know you can't promise me anything, and I'm not asking for anything from you. I'm really not. I panicked because just being near you is becoming so easy that the thought of not having that is overwhelming. I don't know what to do about those feelings.'

'We came into each other's lives at the right time. We've been good for each other, but that doesn't mean it has to be something permanent. Our lives are so different. I just don't see...' He sighed with frustration. 'What I'm saying is that even if we decided that we did want to make this a more permanent arrangement, how would that even be possible? It's not like you'd give up House of Hearts, and I most certainly couldn't live in Rainbow Valley, not with all the early-morning TV work.'

'Don't play the geography card, Simon. You know as well as I do that isn't the issue. You're quite happy having me tucked up in your penthouse, so you can make love whenever the urge strikes, but to have me as your visible partner, well that's a whole different thing, isn't it? Surely it would ruin your reputation if people saw you had a soft side? And where would your credibility go if the woman on your arm was a loony who sells love hearts? You might be able to kid yourself, but you don't fool me, Simon.'

'I brought you out to the yacht to calm you down. I can see that didn't work. Soraya, I like you. I like you a lot. I have no fears about you being seen on my arm. It's you that keeps putting up a wall between us, and suggesting that we're not suited. We have more in common than you think.'

She laughed. 'You think so?'

'You're financially savvy, for a start.'

'Yes, but Simon that doesn't mean we stand on common ground. In fact, it just highlights how different our worldview is. You exist in a financial world based on fear. I take a metaphysical approach to money. See, we're diametrically opposed?'

'What the hell does that mean? Metaphysical? Is this some sort of New-Age claptrap?'

'Your arrogance makes you look ignorant, Simon. Your financial views aren't the only legitimate ones, you know. Quantum physics shows us that money is love.'

When he snickered, she simply dismissed him and continued.

'It's what makes the world go round. Paper, coins, it's all just energy. It only has the power we give it. You, and people like you, infuse it with fear and live with the thought you might lose it. Other people see it as a symbol of the love they put out into the world. They know it will be returned to them in some form.'

Soraya turned away, taking in the view of the harbour.

'You really believe that?' He shook his head in utter disbelief. 'I thought you said you followed my advice about financial well-being?'

'I do. Well, I *did*. Some of your investment advice is sound.'

'Some? Some of it?'

'You are so full of yourself! You might have earned your fortune from handing out financial advice to the rich and famous, and people might hang off your every word, but frankly Simon, even you have to admit that you're not always right.' She stood up, her anger increasing by the second. 'I've had enough of this. We really are miles apart, no matter what you say. Let's put an end to this charade. You've got all the information you need about House of Hearts, assuming you're still going to mention it in your book. There's no need to play nursemaid to me any longer. Take me back to your place. I'll get a bus home.'

'No, Soraya. We've come out for an adventure, and that's what we're doing. If you really want to go home, you can, but only once we've finished here.'

'Simon...'

'Don't argue,' he said, standing up, then holding her close.

'That's it? Don't argue? You think giving me a cuddle is a quick way to silence me?'

'If that doesn't work, maybe this will?'

And he was right. He knew that a simple kiss would have her melting in his arms. Simon hated himself for it, but right now he was desperate. They'd had such a beautiful evening and he didn't want it ruined. What he wanted was simple: another night with Soraya Juniper in his arms. And another. Why did it all have to be so damn complicated? Why did their worlds have to be miles apart, literally and figuratively? What if she lived in New York? Would that have made any difference?

He knew the truth of the matter: it wasn't that their worlds were light years apart. Simon Beaudin simply didn't want to be in a long-term relationship.

They kissed on the deck for about half an hour. Simon was desperate to take her to his room, but thought better of it. Best to get her back on an even keel before going any further.

'I'm sorry,' he said sincerely. 'I didn't mean to sound so dismissive, it's just that you're talking a foreign language.'

'So why don't you just open yourself to the possibility that there is more than one way of looking at money?'

'Okay, okay. Tell me more about money and quantum whatever-it's-called.'

'It's simple, really,' she continued. 'Whatever we focus on, we attract; and the same goes for money. If we expect to increase our income or attract money through other means, it sends a message out into the ethers or Universe or whatever you want to call it. The same works for getting into debt, by the way.'

'What does that mean?' he asked, once again shaking his head in disbelief.

'Well, the universal energy force is constantly listening to us and the messages we send out, so if you're fretting about bills or rent day, then you're not going to draw money to you but repel it.'

'You don't seriously believe this?'

'No, I don't believe it. I *know* it. Money is no different to any other aspect of our life. We have to take

131

responsibility for our feelings. But the truth is that most people don't want that level of power. They want to be victims.'

'Well, on that last point, I might just have to agree,' he laughed.

'If you agree with that, then you have to agree that you increase your wealth by increasing your positive thoughts.'

'When you put it that way, yes, however, if it were that simple then everyone would be rich. So why aren't they?'

'Because most of our beliefs about money are stored in the subconscious! Ninety percent of our lives are governed by stuff we're not even aware of.'

'Have you ever thought about lecturing on this stuff?'

She laughed out loud, and said 'what, and be heckled by people like you? No thanks!'

Soraya snuggled in closer to him grateful to feel some sort of connection despite their differing viewpoints. The last thing she wanted tonight was to be at odds with him.

They sailed for three days along the Eastern seaboard, dining alfresco, laughing, making love, chatting, slow dancing, and visiting seaside towns. Soraya was looking out to sea at a passing yacht.

'Most people say they want to be rich, but they have no idea what wealth looks like to them. Is it another TV or car? Is it an overseas holiday? Perhaps it's living in a condo rather than a house share. It's when people become clear about what wealth means to them personally, and what their life would look like if they had it, then they start attracting it to them.'

Simon laughed. 'So, living in Rainbow Valley in that pretty little doll's house is your idea of wealth?'

'I don't feel poor!' She sat up feeling rather indignant. 'I love where I live. I have land around me. To me, that is wealth. I only ever wanted to be surrounded by nature and to be able to disappear into woodland.'

'I'm sorry, I wasn't judging you. It's just that at the level of wealth you're earning, some people might expect your lifestyle to be different.'

'I have exactly the lifestyle I want.'

'Let me ask you this: why don't you apply the same ideas to relationships? Why didn't you attract a man into your life?'

'I have, actually.'

'I thought we weren't matched?' he laughed.

'Yes, you're right. I just didn't refine my list very well.' She smiled, 'but don't change the subject! We're meant to be talking about money.'

'The same rules apply, though, right?'

'As I was saying,' she said, trying to change the subject back to money. 'Money is a life force. It reflects self-worth and self-care. It's about how we give and receive.' She didn't get to finish the conversation, though, because Simon once again had his arms around her.

'I'd like to give you something,' he said.

'Simon,' she giggled. 'Are you ever going to take me seriously?'

'I do,' he whispered, kissing the nape of her neck. 'I'm taking you so seriously that I want to take you to bed. Let's go!'

Simon slowly undressed Soraya, letting her clothing slip to the floor by the side of their huge bed. She could see the stars twinkling and moonlight shining upon the sea water. This was one of the most luxurious bedrooms she'd ever been in, and right now she felt like a princess.

As she stood naked before him, moonlight splashing across her skin, Simon said 'You're stunning. You look absolutely gorgeous.'

'Shall I undress you?' she asked softly, her hands reaching to unbutton his shirt.

'Not yet,' his voice was barely a rasp, as he reached for her hands and placed them by her side. 'I just want to admire you, here, like this.' His breathing was ragged now, as his hands moved slowly from her bare, slender shoulders down to her breasts. Simon allowed himself the luxury of letting his hands be filled with her ample and malleable breasts. They were softer than pillows, and Simon wanted to bury his head there forever. *Forever*.

He fell to his knees, and looked up at her, silently worshipping every inch of her beautiful body. She was a Goddess, to him, and he wanted her to feel worshipped.

As Simon's hands moved from her hips down to her thighs, he heard her slight whimper. Perhaps now she'd be less agitated and determined to prove their differences. Perhaps now they'd find a common ground that they could both recognise.

Soraya felt his fingers trace the inside of her thigh, and an involuntary quiver had her sighing.

'I can't stand,' she moaned. 'My legs feel weak. Simon? I need to sit or lie down. I...'

To him, she always smelt so damned good: like Summer rain or honey with beeswax. Simon wanted more of her, and he wanted her now.

'I can't stand, I really can't...'

He moved her onto the bed, and lay her back, with her legs hung over the bed. Simon kneeled on the floor.

'Your sighs are muted today, what's wrong?' he asked tenderly, and slightly confused. Their eyes met across her olive-skinned breasts. 'Are you not enjoying this?'

'I don't want anyone to hear me.'

'No one is going to hear you, I promise!' he laughed. 'Only I can hear you. Let me hear you, honey. Let me hear you. I love the sounds you make when I'm loving you like this.'

The pleasure was excruciating, and Soraya wasn't sure how much more she could take.

'You are the most beautiful woman in the world. I can't get enough of you, Soraya. God you're gorgeous!'

Simon slowly released a contented groan. It was the sound of a man about to walk to nirvana.

That familiar bubbling up of intense pleasure felt like a luxury money could never buy. As they crossed to the other side, simultaneously tortured and elated, they gave themselves fully to each other. They tumbled into bliss, sated and sexually satisfied.

They stayed in bed for a couple of hours, kissing, and stroking each other's back.

'Why aren't you married?' Soraya asked out of the blue. She didn't know what possessed her, but it was too late. The words were out. She couldn't take them back, and there was no point in apologising.

When he didn't answer, she removed her head from his chest and made eye contact.

'Marriage is like money, Soraya. It's something you invest in, and you have to do it carefully and wisely!

You invest time, energy, and you have to compromise a huge and vital part of who you are in order to make a marriage successful.'

'And love? Does love come into the equation? Or is it all about a contract to you?' She felt herself become agitated. How could he say something so…so *heartless*, when they'd just made love?

'I had never met anyone that I wanted to invest my time, energy or *love* into like that. Marriage isn't something you agree to in the first moments of heated passion with someone. Soraya, I've never met anyone who invested wisely by getting married. By falling in love. It's just something that has never made sense to me.'

'So when you're making love to me, what is that? Just wild, crazy sex? Don't tell me that it is, because I know it's not! I know that your heart is opening every time we're together in this way. Why are you pretending otherwise?'

'I'm not pretending, and I wasn't talking about you. You asked why I wasn't married, and I was talking about my life before you came along.'

She wrapped a sheet around her naked body, and hobbled to the ensuite.

'Soraya,' he called after her, but it was no use. She was angry. It hadn't been his intention to upset her. It never was! Simon had just wanted to answer honestly. The truth was he'd never met anyone, until now, that he felt was worth investing his whole life in. But he hadn't got that far into the conversation. He hadn't had a chance to feel like he could share that with her. Of course he wanted to be with her. Simon couldn't imagine not being with her, but it was too soon, surely, to make that sort of commitment? Either way, she wasn't prepared to listen anymore to what he had to say.

If she was going to be angry, it was probably best to get out of her way for a while.

After she was dressed, Soraya avoided eye contact and went to the library at the far end of the yacht.

Simon showered, and then headed up to the open deck. He needed fresh air. How was it possible to spend hours making love to someone only to end up having an argument? It drove him crazy. *She* drove him crazy! He thumped a wall in frustration. Simon hated it when they misunderstood each other. If there was anything he knew about their relationship it was that it didn't have to be so fraught with tension. So why did they keep ending up in this place? For some time, he paced the deck trying to find a way to make it up to Soraya. How could he begin to explain that she was most definitely worth investing in? That, actually, there was nothing else he could think about but spending a very long time with her. Yes, he wanted to invest time, love, energy and money into their relationship. And tonight he'd tell her. Once and for all they'd come to a resolution and could finally enjoy a more peaceful relationship. He had to wait until she calmed down, first. Simon acknowledged quietly to himself that she was worth waiting for.

The captain approached Simon, the furrowed brown on his face, a sign of trouble ahead.

'Have you heard the news at all? I'm afraid we need to return to shore. There's a violent storm forecast. I've been keeping an eye on it. I had hoped we might avoid it altogether. You don't want this beautiful vessel tossed about at sea.'

Simon was interrupted by the ring of his cell phone.

'Simon Beaudin.' He was quiet for a moment, then said 'Yes, okay. Tomorrow at noon is fine.'

Simon instructed the captain to turn the yacht around, and head back in the direction of land.

'Still not talking to me?' he asked when Soraya came on deck.

'Of course I'm talking to you. I'm just fed up, that's all. I don't want to fight with you. I like you, Simon, but everything about this is too complicated. I don't want complicated in my life. I'm not interested in being part of a fling or half-hearted relationship. Not with you, not with anyone.'

Simon refrained from laughing at the intense brow furrowing up on her pretty little face.

'I know.' He reached over and touched her hand, a silent truce forming between them. Simon's face grew concerned as he monitored the dark clouds hovering over the city skyline. 'That storm is coming in earlier than was first forecast. It's probably best if you wait in the cabin.'

'I'm okay out here. I don't think it will rain before we get back into harbour.'

Simon was in no mood to argue, and decided to make small talk.

'That was my editor calling earlier. He's arranged a journalist to interview me tomorrow about my book. The publishing house wants to get the ball rolling before it's published, you know, to put the taste of it out there.'

'How much of the book will you share?'

'Nothing really, just a sense of the impact a recession has on even the most robust businesses, and a few secrets of the trade.'

And that's how they continued their sail back into the harbour. Small talk. Lots of irrelevant small talk. They both avoided the topic of marriage and investment, and the fact they'd had an argument about it.

The winds were brutal, the waters choppy. Soraya listened as the waves smashed up against the sides of the yacht, symbolic of the way she'd been feeling since their heated exchange earlier.

'Why don't you wait in the harbourside café while I help Max and the crew get everything closed up here?'

'No. I'm more than capable of helping.'

Simon couldn't help but smile at her hobbling about on the plastered leg, fighting the gale-force winds.

When Simon finally secured *My Darling*, he wrapped his coat around Soraya, and held her hand. 'Come on, let's get out of this. It's going to get a lot worse.'

An hour later, freezing cold, they both sank into the sofa, relieved to be out of the storm. The first snowflakes of the season skittered about in the violent winds. The bleak pewter clouds menaced the city skyline, a promise of the long night ahead. Soraya was still angry, and he knew it. Simon thought about the first day they met, and couldn't help but chuckle to himself that she had such a multi-faceted personality. One thing was for sure: she kept him on his toes. Simon was growing to like the fact that her moods could be unpredictable. At least their relationship would never be boring.

'I'll get a cab to the bus depot. There's no need for you to escort me there.'

'Soraya.' If there was anything he'd learnt from his mother, it was the importance of giving someone the freedom to do what they needed to do; he wasn't going to beg her to stay.

'Don't Soraya me. It's time for me to go, you know that as well as I do. You've got everything you need from me for your book. There's no point in extending my stay.'

'Your leg.'

'I'll manage. I'm already moving about more confidently. I can arrange my working day so that I have everything I need on ground level.'

'You really want to go back?' Simon was desperately hoping that she was bluffing, and that she'd stay.

'It's for the best. For both of us. You know that as well as I do.'

Was there any point in arguing with her? She was right: he had what he needed. Well, almost.

'Let me check what time the next bus leaves. There's no point sitting in a draughty bus depot any longer than you have to. I'm happy to drive you back, you know. You don't have to be so stubborn.'

'No thanks,' she said, gathering some of her items from the dining table. Soraya looked up as the violent, snow-laden winds lashed the windows.

Simon logged onto his laptop and searched online for the bus timetable. 'Slight problem, Soraya. All public transport in and out of New York has been cancelled. This is going to be a big storm. They're calling it a Superstorm with up to ten inches of snow forecast overnight.'

'Fine. Fine! You can drive me then.'

'Have you heard anything I've just said? There is

140

a risk to life. This isn't an April shower we're talking about here, Soraya. It won't kill you to stay another night or two. We've managed this long.'

Simon watched her shiver, unable to determine if it was the chill in the room or her angst at not getting her own way. 'I'll turn the heating up, and put the fire on. It'll be toasty warm in no time.'

Soraya stood at the window for several minutes, alarmed at the rapidly decreasing visibility of the city lights, and conceded that perhaps it wasn't the best idea in the world to undertake a four-hour road trip. She sat down at her laptop, and immersed herself in the final touches of the manuscript. If she was going to be stuck here for another night, she may as well put the time to good use and give her script a final proofread; then she could email it to her publisher.

'Would you mind if I use your printer?' she asked, aware of 'needing' him yet again.

'Be my guest,' he smiled, realising how hard it must have been for her to ask a favour. Then he picked up her laptop, and carried it for her.' Simon opened the door to his writing studio, and then headed back to the kitchen. 'I'll just make us a bite to eat. Call me if you need anything. There's plenty of paper on the shelf to the right.'

Soraya changed the settings on her laptop to accommodate the alien printer, then set her document up to print, and stared out at the shrouded city. How did this happen, she asked herself. When did life get so complicated? Simon Beaudin was everything she didn't need in a man. And yet, and yet she couldn't get him out her head, or out of her heart. The sooner she returned home, the better. For both of them. Time would erase his memory, and the scent of his skin, the feel of his strong hands against the small of her back, his breath against her neck. Time would erase everything.

Soraya stacked the printed papers and placed them neatly beside the printer as she packed up her laptop. No matter what she did, it was impossible to get the image of them making love out of her head, and a heaviness crept over her at the thought of never doing that again.

'Your cellphone is ringing, Soraya,' Simon called from the kitchen. 'Shall I answer it for you?'

'Yes!' She picked up her laptop, and hobbled back to the open-plan dining room.

'Yes, Santana, she's just fine. We're safe from the storm. She's here now, if you'd like to talk to her.'

'Hey sis,' she said after taking the phone from his hands, all the while avoiding eye contact, but when his skin brushed hers, the both felt it: that spark of electricity that they were desperately trying to deny. Who were they trying to fool? The sexual chemistry between them was as alive and tense as ever.

'Actually I'll be home soon, Santana. Tomorrow, maybe, if the buses are running.'

She paused for a moment. 'Really, everything is just fine. I'm able to look after myself now. Honestly, don't give it another thought. I'll call you when I'm home. Love you.'

'So you didn't want to tell her that I'm driving you crazy, and that you can't wait to see the back of me?'

'I never said that, Simon.'

'You implied it.'

'You do drive me crazy. Everything about you unhinges me! I have no shame in admitting that.'

'And yet,' he said, coming close to her, his hand gently cupping her chin, 'as I recall you rather enjoyed being unhinged.'

'There's more to a relationship than just good sex!' She tried turning away, but he secured her to the spot.

'Yes, there is.'

Simon leaned forward, and within seconds that familiar tango of their mouths had them reaching under each other's shirts, desperate, oh so desperate, for the feel and smell of bare skin.

The phone stopped them both.

Startled, Soraya pulled away as if she'd just been rescued from a danger zone.

'Simon Beaudin.'

He looked at her as if not concentrating fully on the caller, then dipped his eyes to focus on what was being said. It was impossible to concentrate on anything when he was looking at her and mentally undressing every last item of clothing from her body.

Simon sighed, as if being forced to do something against his will. 'Yes, I suppose that would be alright. Come on over.' He hung up the phone.

'I'm sorry, I had hoped to spend your last night here doing something a little more pleasant, but the journalist wants to come over now because he fears he won't be able to walk through the snow in the morning. Do you mind?'

'Why would I mind? We won't be having sex again, if that's what you were planning.'

'Soraya? Is it so wrong to enjoy each other's bodies?'

'I want more than that! More!'

'But you said…'

'Never mind what I said! I don't want to just be someone's time-filler. I don't want to be in someone's life just because there's no one else on the scene for them. How do you think that makes me feel?'

'It's not like that at all, Soraya. You know it's not. Come here.'

'No!' she said, walking away.

'You realise I can outrun you, right?' And that mischievous smile which had captivated her from the first morning they met, had her laughing out loud.

When she turned around, Soraya asked 'And what are you going to do, Mr Beaudin, throw me over your shoulders?'

'How about my knee?' He closed the space between them. 'If you're going home, at least let's part on good terms. Okay?'

'Good terms does not mean *sex*.'

'We can talk about that later,' he winked, 'but first, let's eat before this journo gets here.'

She was taken completely by surprise when Simon scooped her up and carried her to the dining table. 'Simon!' she squealed.

'Just letting you know who has the upper hand here,' he laughed, then slowly leaned in to kiss her. 'Tell me that you're not going to miss that.'

Her eyes were closed, as if she'd been drugged. When she didn't answer, he knew exactly how much she would miss his kisses. An ache gnawed in the depths of his belly, growling louder than hunger pangs. The penthouse would feel so empty without her here and he tried to banish the thought. It just didn't make sense. Life was good before she came along. Wonderfully good. Wasn't it?

Simon carefully placed Soraya on her feet, and pulled out a dining chair for her. 'I'll be back in a jiffy,' he promised, entering the kitchen just as the cooking timer buzzed.

'This looks gorgeous,' she said, breathing in the aroma. 'I didn't realize how hungry I was! What is it?'

'Eggplant timbale with goat's cheese. It's stacked with roasted zucchini, tomatoes, and infused with garlic and fresh basil.

'I could eat like this every day!'

'You do! I've eaten your cooking, remember?'

'Yes, but it always tastes different when someone else prepares your food.'

'So you like being nurtured?'

Their eyes caught. He'd touched a sore spot. It was clear that she spent her days looking after other people, and rarely had someone to fuss over her. And that's when it hit Simon: that's why she wants to leave! Being protected, comforted and cared for was so far out of her comfort zone. No wonder she had a panic attack. That's when he realised that it wasn't the future she was scared about, but the present.

'I will miss taking care of you when you're gone, Soraya.' His words were gentle, and his tone tender.

'I'm sure you'll slip back into your bachelor ways pretty quickly,' she said.

'Soraya, you are a woman worth investing in. I...'

The buzzer to the penthouse rang, startling them both.

'He's early. Damn!' Simon was furious. He was about to tell her that if ever there was a woman he

145

would be willing to put time, energy and *love* into, it was her: Soraya Juniper.

'It's okay.'

Simon apologised, and went to let him in.

'Simon Beaudin, good evening. I'm Jorge Perez. Pleased to meet you. Your reputation extends far and wide. It's a career high for me to interview you. Thank you,' he said, flicking off the snowflakes from his duffle coat before stepping inside.

'No problem. I'm afraid you've just caught us finishing our meal. Could you give us a few moments?'

'I'm so sorry, of course I can.' Jorge passed his coat to Simon, and then followed him into the open-plan dining area.

'This is Soraya Juniper. She's the owner of one of the businesses featured in my book. Soraya, this is Jorge.'

'Pleased to meet you.' She looked him up and down, and something inside shifted gears. Maybe it was women's intuition, but she didn't like the guy. Not one bit. It wasn't as if he were ugly or creepy in any way that was physically repugnant; it was something that went way beyond words.

'Jorge, perhaps you could make yourself comfortable in my writing room?' Simon said, leading the way. 'I'll be with you in about five minutes. Can I get you a coffee?'

'Lovely. Black, two sugars.'

Once he was out of earshot, Simon said 'We can finish our conversation later.'

'Simon, there's no need. Really. We've said everything that needs to be said. Thank you for a perfect meal.'

'Perfect?'

'Yes,' she laughed. 'Perfect. It's certainly not the strangest meal I've ever had,' she said, standing up.

'And what was that?'

'What?' she asked, losing the direction of their conversation.

'What's the strangest meal you've ever had?' Simon laughed.

Soraya looked him firmly in the eyes, and without batting an eyelid said: 'The heart of a cheating ex-lover!'

Simon had no idea whether she was serious or not. The woman only ate vegetables, surely she wouldn't... No, she must have been joking. Why didn't the expression on her face change?

'Is there anything else I can get you?' he asked.

'No, thanks. I'm ready to sleep. See you in the morning.'

Jorge was a rigorous interviewer, leaving no stone unturned, but when he started asking questions about Soraya, Simon felt himself bristling.

'If you don't mind, please keep the questions focused on the businesses themselves, and not the owners. Their private lives aren't up for discussion.'

'But our readers will be curious to know more about them, like what they do in their spare time, what hobbies they have, and if they do any other work.'

'Soraya is the owner of House of Hearts. Focus on the business, please.'

Jorge continued to probe.

'Have you interviewed all the subjects of your book here, in your home?'

Simon stood up, furious. 'I met Ms Juniper in her place of business. She broke her leg, and I offered for her to stay here. End of story.'

'So you're not in a relationship with Ms Juniper, because that would be a conflict of interest for your book, wouldn't it? Promoting a business when you're sleeping with the proprietor wouldn't come across very well to your fans.'

'Mr Perez, you're way off the mark. This interview is over! Let me show you to the door.'

Simon stormed across the room. 'My publisher will be contacting your editor. There will be no article about me or my book in your publication!'

'If you've got nothing to hide, then there's no issue, is there?' Jorge was like a dog with a bone, his growl as threatening as his demeanour. 'You've not even attempted to deny there's anything going on.'

'Why should I deny it? You've seen a man and a woman sharing a meal, and made assumptions. The problem is yours, not mine.'

'Do you normally dine by candlelight with people you're interviewing?'

'Mr Perez. Enough. Leave.'

With the door firmly closed behind him, Simon leaned against the wall, his pulse rapid and his thoughts wired. Despite the late hour, he had to call his publisher straight away.

'Eric, I need a favour. Pull the plug on that interview. The guy was an idiot. I don't want anything going in the New York Times written by that fool.'

'Leave it with me,' Eric said.

Simon paced the dining room for some time. The last thing he wanted to do was to wake Soraya, and yet his first instinct, his strongest desire, was to hold her in his arms. Scum like Jorge Perez could cause no end of damage with their speculation.

Simon brewed himself another coffee, and decided to finish the final chapter of his book.

> Juniper takes a unique attitude to money, and I've learnt more than I ever expected. I approached her with scepticism, and, quite frankly, arrogance. Her thriving business is evidence of money being a force for good in a world which continues to perpetuate that it is the root of all evil. Her dynamic quantum-physics take on money, if applied to mainstream businesses, could transform the market place, erasing the word 'recession' from our vocabulary.

As Simon typed THE END, he felt a huge sense of relief but also disappointment. Of all times, this was a cause for celebration. The book was finally finished! Soon he could go back to working on the newspaper, and doing his daily TV and radio presenting. Yes, things would be back to normal. So why didn't he feel overjoyed?

When he switched on the printer, his eyes caught sight of Soraya's manuscript. The title page read: *Love*

*Never Dies* by Ashley Starr. Simon's heart raced. Was it autobiographical? Although he wanted to read her novel, somehow the thought of going through those pages was akin to reading someone's diary: he had no right.

While Simon's manuscript was printing, he bound Soraya's pages together in a thick rubber band, and then took it to the dining room and placed it by her laptop. She'd be gone tomorrow, if the transport was running. *Gone.*

'So, this is it?' he said, two days later when the storm diminished, holding her hand as the icy winds rattled through the bus depot. 'Are you sure I can't drive you?'

'Perfectly sure. Simon? Thank you for everything. I mean it. Thank you.'

'You don't have to leave,' he said, drawing in closer to her.

'I do. You know I do. This has taken us both to a place neither of us wants to be. It's incompatible with our lifestyles.'

Simon searched her eyes hoping to find a sign that perhaps they could find a way to reside in each other's hearts.

'You know where I am if you change your mind.' Reluctantly, he kissed her on the cheek as the bus driver placed her luggage onboard. 'Goodbye Soraya.'

# Home

Despite having only been away from Simon for less than twenty four hours, Soraya was missing him terribly. There was only one thing for it: work. Quite quickly, she managed to negotiate the staircase, but the ascent meant sitting on her bottom and lifting herself up, one step at a time. Still, she felt terribly proud of herself for making a few dozen gingerbread hearts. *Home*, she said to herself. *I'm home*.

Soraya hobbled around the shop, placing new items that had been in storage onto the shelves. Hearts made from sea rope, mosaic, mirror, bookends, photo frames. Soraya stopped at the bookshelves, admiring her latest release. 'Good work, girl', she said out loud, then headed to the front door, and placed the 'open, come inside' sign.

Soraya had set herself a goal to write a list of fifty things that money couldn't buy, and then send it in a love-heart-shaped wallet to Simon.

And so her list began: a positive attitude; a golden wedding anniversary; best friends; trust; natural beauty; happy children; a strong work ethic; good ideas; a good-hair day; appreciation; life purpose. She kept writing, saving her favourite till last: *true love*. When the postman dropped off the mail that morning, she filled his hands with the package. For the past week, she had been thinking of this list, and felt rather pleased with herself at finally having committed it to paper.

Was Simon happy, she wondered. Really happy?

It was all very well being in his penthouse with expansive views over the city, but were they more enjoyable because he was on his own?

Surely they'd mean more if he had someone to share them with? If he had her to share them with?

Soraya was in a daydream thinking back to the first time they made love on the slipper chair, the afternoon sunlight streaming through the large windows. She sighed. Had it really happened? One look at her plastered leg and she became acutely aware that none of it was a dream.

It seemed as if everyone in Rainbow Valley paid a visit that morning, not just for their beloved cookies, but to buy a heart 'for a friend' they said. Customers were most concerned about the loss of trade she'd endured, and showed their solidarity with a purchase. Soraya was grateful to be home, and back to reality. Simon was never far from her thoughts; the memory of his words and touch lingered alongside every breath she took.

Just before closing for lunch, there was a courier delivery. As she signed for the packet, her mind raced: *It's so small. I haven't ordered single items.*

Opening the packet, she found a love-heart-shaped pin cushion with two thick pins inserted, and a handwritten note:

> *Don't let the pain of past loves*
> *stop your heart from opening up*
> *to new possibilities.*
> *Thinking of you, Simon.*

*A pin cushion?* He thinks my heart is a pin cushion!

Fury stopped her from registering the face of the next customer. 'I'll be with you in a moment,' she called out without looking up again.

Already she was mentally preparing the conversation that she'd have with Simon when she phoned him at lunchtime. It would go something like this: 'I choose the hearts, not you!' And with that thought, she placed the heart back into the package, angry that he considered hers to be permanently stabbed. How dare he! My heart is damn fine, thank you very much!

Soraya looked up, and it took several seconds to place where she knew the face from. It was out of context, and she felt disoriented.

'Jorge? Jorge Perez, isn't it?' she asked, that uncomfortable feeling she had when they met, rising like bile. 'What brings you all the way out here? You're a long way from home.'

'Miss Juniper,' he said, reaching to shake her hand.

Soraya declined. It was most out of character, but she couldn't dismiss the warning bells. Whatever the reason, she didn't trust the guy. The feeling was visceral. So deep, so primal, that she couldn't find words, but one thing was sure: she always trusted her gut instinct.

'Just following up on a story, actually. I was rather intrigued by Mr Beaudin's passion for your business. I wanted to see it for myself.'

'You drove four hours to see it for yourself? You couldn't take his word for it?'

Jorge didn't answer, but started wandering around the store.

The man's energy was toxic, and she wanted him out. Not once, not a single time, in all the years of owning House of Hearts had she experienced such a primeval reaction to a customer. But he wasn't a customer, was he? Jorge was here to snoop.

'What do you need to know? I'm about to close for lunch. I'm happy to answer any of your questions.'

Not once did he look up at her but continued to examine every item in the shop. Jorge stopped by the bookshelf and started smiling. He flipped through the latest release. *What, he's pretending to like romance novels? Jerk!*

'I really need to close up now.'

He barely looked at her, and grinned as he headed to the door. 'Of course. I'll be on my way. Have a good day!'

*That's it? He drives four hours, and then disappears again?*

She watched him outside, fiddling with something, and then he began to take photos of House of Hearts. Soray's heart sank. Why House of Hearts? Why was he so keen to feature this business on his profile of Simon?

When Jorge got in the rental car and drove away, Soraya locked the front door. Taken aback, her heart was beating like the wings of a hummingbird, and that sick feeling was still there, washing over her like a flood.

As she neared the front counter, she spied the packet from Simon, and a smile made its way to her face. Despite the message of the heart, his intentions were good. Oh how she missed him!

Soraya bottom-stepped her way up the staircase. She'd phone Simon to say thank you, and tell him about that creep Jorge turning up.

'Simon Beaudin.' His mellifluous tone caught her off guard. It was so good to hear his voice again. Though he was hundreds of miles away, in this moment it was like he was right there, with his arms around her.

'Cute heart,' she said, not introducing herself. 'I'm sure it will come in handy.'

'Your heart is far too precious to keep those pins in it, you know. They don't have to be permanently embedded.'

'Ah, Mr Beaudin the wise man!'

They both laughed, and then the silence which fell

154

was long but comfortable. Oh so comfortable.

'I'm missing you,' he whispered, his voice hoarse. 'I'm missing you so much. Far more than I imagined was possible.'

'Me too.'

They chatted about this and that, and nothing at all, and everything. Everything, that is, except Jorge Perez. Somehow, just hearing Simon's voice, made that man's recent visit completely leave her mind.

'Soraya, I want to see you again. May I drive up on the weekend?'

There was a silence, and she wondered if she might say no. Could this really be the end for them?

'I'd like that very much. Simon?'

'Yes.'

'I can't wait. The weekend seems so far away.'

# Double Life

Soraya arose early, despite the darkness, and began baking several dozen cookies for the shop, and a cake for when Simon came. As she busied herself in the kitchen, she hummed a tune. For a while, she felt like a lovesick teenager, lifting her apron skirt and dancing around the room, singing an old Patsy Cline song. Damn, had she fallen in love? Irrevocably in love with Simon Beaudin? So this is what it feels like? Soraya laughed out loud.

At 9.45 she headed downstairs to prepare the shop before opening. Saturdays were always the busiest day, with tourists flocking in to the valley.

To her surprise, the front verandah of House of Hearts was filled with people, and there were cars and vans on the road for as far as the eye could see. What on Earth was going on?

Saturdays were busy, but never this busy. It was probably best to open up now rather than leave people standing in the icy wind for another fifteen minutes. As soon as she unlocked the front door, staccato-style camera flashes bombarded her from left to right.

Soraya covered her eyes, but couldn't move fast enough. People were pushing right by her into the shop.

'Is it true, Ms Juniper, that you're the novelist Ashley Starr?'

'Ashley Starr, what's it like living a double life?'

'Were you ever going to reveal your true identity?'

'How long have you and Simon Beaudin been an item?'

'Are you getting married?'

The questions came thick and fast, and she was surrounded at all sides by cameras, by strange men and women, and by relentless questions.

Soraya couldn't find her voice. It was stuck, somewhere in the bottom of her throat, desperately trying to find a way up but unable to move. And then her mind was awash with images, and she felt hands on her shoulders helping her to move away. Two local policemen started ordering the crowd out of the shop.

Sam Gentry, a thirty-year-old policeman who'd been serving in Rainbow Valley for five years, came up to her after the last journalist was pushed out the front door.

'Are you okay, Soraya? What the hell just happened here? We were doing a routine patrol when we saw the satellite vans, and whole street filled with cars.'

Soraya couldn't answer; her hands were shaking, and tears slipped from her eyes. Sam helped her to a chair. 'Sit down. Jeff,' he said to the other policeman on duty, 'Run down to Mable's Coffee House and pick up a few coffees. We're going to need them.' Then he turned back to Soraya. 'Shall I phone Santana? Your folks? Anyone? Soraya, talk to me. I know you're in shock, but I can't help you if you don't tell me what you need.'

She looked up at him, almost as if she wasn't in her body, but looking down over the whole proceedings.

'How did they know?' Her voice was barely a squeak.

'How did they know what?' he asked. 'I don't know what you're talking about.'

They sat in silence for five minutes. Numb with shock, Soraya was unable to speak.

Jeff returned with coffees and cake.

'Take a look at this,' he said to Sam, passing him a copy of the New York Times.

'Oh, I see.' Sam started laughing. 'I'm not laughing

at what's just happened, I promise. I'm laughing that you've had us fooled for all these years.' Then, in a serious voice, he apologised. 'I'm sorry, what's happened this morning is traumatic. You're a famous novelist? No way.' He shook his head in disbelief.

'I don't understand how this happened. Nobody knew...nobody except my parents and Santana... and...'

No, it wasn't possible. Simon would never tell. Would he? How dare he? Surely he knew that she trusted him with her life? This was such a betrayal of everything they'd shared in recent weeks.

Maybe he really was a man whose heart was made of money? Maybe he'd exposed her to Jorge for a substantial fee? That had to be it! There was no other possible explanation. Well he couldn't come and visit now! Any chance of them having a relationship, no matter how brief, was completely off the cards. Betrayal was a road she'd been down before, and there was no way any man had a second chance once he'd broken her confidence.

'I need to be alone, gentlemen. I'm sorry. Thank you for your help. I'll keep the shop closed today. Here,' she said, 'take these cookies. They'll just go to waste otherwise.'

Their eyes lit up. 'Look, we'll call the station and arrange to have officers stay out front for a few days while this calms down. Keep your head down, okay?'

Soraya nodded, and as they left she allowed herself to cry. Every heartache of her life splashed down her red cheeks. All the pain and wounds of the heart cascading before her eyes. For the first time in all these years, Soraya regretted not having curtains or shutters on the front windows and door. The transparency of the shop front amplified her wholehearted belief that 'what you see is what you get'; but today, she could see the irony. She'd been living a double life for so long that she never gave it much thought. Of course people would be shocked. Would they expect something different from her now? Would people stop buying her books? How would House of Hearts survive this exposé?

Simon. Simon Beaudin. Rotten, lousy, money-hungry scoundrel! How dare he! Soraya yelled with fury, and knew that she had to bottom-shuffle up those stairs pronto. There was no other option but to phone him and tell him never to come near her again. Not today. Not any day!

It took two minutes to get up that wretched staircase, and every second seemed more like an hour. Soraya had never felt such anger. Well, at least not since finding out about Stephen. 'Men!' she cursed. 'I hate them. I hate all of them!'

After ten attempts at calling Simon's landline, she tried his cellphone. He couldn't have left New York already, surely? He'd said he wasn't leaving till later in the day. No matter what, she had to stop him. The last thing she wanted—or *needed*—was to see him. That would be too distracting, and she wouldn't put it past him to try and sweet-talk his way out of it.

No, she had to keep a distance between them. It was the only way she'd be able to think straight.

Soraya screamed. She didn't care if half the valley heard her. She was angry. So angry, she could…

Why would he do that? Why would Simon betray her confidence like that? Sure, they were diametrically opposed in so many ways, but this? This was the ultimate betrayal. There was no coming back from something as fundamentally wrong as breaking someone's trust.

What did he hope to achieve? Was he trying to prove a point?

No wonder Jorge Perez looked so bloody smug. He probably couldn't believe his luck. Scoop of the year. That's what it was to him. Something to feather his nest, and take him to the next echelon of his grubby career path! And her? What did it mean for her?

Life would never be the same again. No longer would she be seen as the sage-like woman with the quaint shop dishing out hearts like a fairy godmother sprinkling gold dust.

Her whole life hung in the balance. Who was she? Who was she really? Was she Ashley Starr or Soraya Juniper? Was she really both? All these years of invisibly balancing her identities, and now the scale was tipped.

Soraya's shaking hands made it hard to read the newspaper article:

```
         Writer of soft porn for women
                living double life
              as homely shopkeeper
               while secretly dating
          Good Morning's Financial Guru
```

'It's not soft porn. They're love stories! It's passion. It's love. It's romance!' she yelled. 'You idiot!'

Soraya sat on her bed, crying until her eyes were red raw. This ranked as one of the three worst days of her life. And once again, it was all because of a man! A stupid, bloody, selfish man!

What the hell do you know about love? Nothing. Nothing at all! *Romance novelist*, she scoffed and threw a small marble statue of Venus, the Goddess of Love, at her bedroom mirror. It splintered and shattered across the floor. That feeling of physical power expressing her deepest anger felt good. Demons unleashed.

'Everything...' she yelled at her angry reflection, 'everything you've ever done has all been wasted! You're a fraud. No one will ever believe anything you have to say again! I hate you Soraya Juniper! Ashley Starr! Whoever the bloody hell you are! I hate you.'

Every item of clothing was ripped from the wardrobe, photo frames flung across the floor; chaos destroyed her beautiful bedroom.

Sobbing and screaming, she bashed her plastered leg against the floorboards until the pain of her life became so overwhelming that she couldn't take it anymore.

# Space

'Santana, it's Simon Beaudin. We have an emergency on our hands.'

'Oh my god, what's happened? Is Soraya okay? I thought she was back at the shop?'

'She's back. Can you meet me there? I might need backup.'

'What are you talking about?' she asked.

'Long story short: the New York Times has exposed her as Ashley Starr. Haven't you seen the article?'

'What? What? How the hell did that happen? Why would you…'

'It wasn't me! Of course it wasn't me. What do you take me for? I'm not a mongrel!' Simon said.

'But no one else would say anything!'

'I promise you, it wasn't me. Just meet me at House of Hearts. I'm about ten minutes away from the valley.'

'I'll be there.'

'Oh crap,' Simon muttered as he approached the main street choked with media. 'Oh God.'

He had no idea how he was going to get to the shop, let alone get in without causing more of a media scrum. Simon phoned Santana to warn her.

'I'm going to leave my car at the bridge, and head up through the woods, and I'll meet you at the back door.

'I think I'll do the same thing. Oh Simon,' she cried. 'Soraya will be terrified. She hates crowds, and she hates unnecessary attention. This will devastate her. Are you sure…'

'Of course I'm sure. You have my word on this. I didn't breathe a word of this to anyone.'

'Okay, I believe you. I can't promise that Soraya

will. I swear, even her best friend doesn't know.'

'I'll see you up there!'

Simon retreated into the woodland. Trees had lost their leaves, leaving little camouflage and he cursed himself for wearing a red jumper. Of all days! So many thoughts raced through his mind. Over and over, he retraced the day of the interview with Jorge Perez, remembering every last word. There was nothing—not a single thing— that could have possibly given him any idea that Soraya wrote as Ashley Starr.

Moving carefully, to make sure no one saw him, within minutes he was near the back of the building. He'd noticed the policemen out front keeping the hoards away from the verandah. Police tape marked off the property, making it clear to everyone concerned that trespassing would not be tolerated.

Simon nearly jumped out of his skin when Santana tapped him on the shoulder. 'Here, let me open the door. I can't believe these crowds. The valley doesn't ever get this busy, not even at festival time.'

Simon followed her inside, with Santana calling Soraya's name throughout the shop.

'Ray? Ray? Where are you? It's me, San. Are you okay?' She turned to Simon. 'I guess she's upstairs. Come on!'

They found her, lifeless, on the bedroom floor. Her hair was dishevelled, and the room looked like an earthquake had struck. Simon stood, motionless, unable to comprehend the scene before him. 'Is she...'

'Yes, she's alive,' Santana assured him, her fingers against her twin sister's pulse. 'Knowing San, she probably screamed herself into exhaustion.'

'She does this often, then?' he asked, concerned, as they both crouched down beside her.

Santana raised her eyebrows. 'No, of course not! Well, maybe once or twice. But not without good reason. Ray,' she whispered, lifting her sister's head into her lap. 'We're here honey, you're safe now. You're safe. No one is going to hurt you.'

It was another five minutes before Soraya gained consciousness. The first face she saw was Simon's.

'Get out! Get out of my house! I don't want you here. I never want to see you again. Get out!' As she tried sitting up, Santana kept her pinned against her chest.

'It wasn't Simon. He said it wasn't him, and I believe him,' Santana said, her voice as firm as her words.

'It had to be. There's no other way. You and mum and dad would never say anything. Simon is the only other person who knew! Get out!'

'I'm not leaving, Soraya. It wasn't me, and if you want me to leave, I will, but not until I prove to you that I'm not responsible for this.'

Soraya sobbed into her sister's arms. 'Everything's ruined, now. I can't ever open these doors again. People would come here for the wrong reasons.'

Santana said 'You don't need to think about any of that right now. All that matters is getting you back on solid ground. Simon, go and make us all a cup of tea.'

When he looked at her blankly, she said 'Or coffee!'

Simon followed her instruction, and as he stood in Soraya's kitchen he thought back to that first day. The day which changed his life forever. And then he recalled his conversation with Gemma, from the newspaper office: 'I know it doesn't make sense, but trust me on this Simon. Please. You won't regret it, and I dare say it might just change your life.'

It was true. Soraya Juniper had changed his life. She'd changed it before she even said her first words to him. She changed it when she walked up the stairs in her pink socks to fetch him coffee. She changed his life when she sang to Alice and Murray. She changed his life when she went tumbling down the stairs. And she changed his life that day on the slipper chair when she opened herself to him. The day they crossed a threshold and became one. It was a day they'd never return from. The day which changed both their lives forever.

The thought of her in the next room, sobbing her heart out until she passed out with exhaustion, shocked him to the core. Had he been responsible for that in *any* way? One thing was for sure: he had to track down Jorge Perez and find out who the hell his source was!

As the milk heated on the stove, he took out his cellphone.

'Jorge, it's Simon Beaudin. Got yourself a little scoop, I see. Clever tack, if you ask me.'

Jorge laughed. 'Well, when my editor said I wasn't allowed to write a story on your book, I wasn't the least bit bothered. I knew this story was way bigger. Thanks for changing my life!' he laughed. 'I'm gonna be a rich man! Ha. Just like you!'

'But I never told you. How the hell did you know?'

'I saw a manuscript written by Ashley Starr in your office. I figured you weren't likely to be working as a novelist, not given your hectic schedule, so it only left one other person.'

Jorge hung up: no word of apology, see you around, or goodbye.

Simon was furious. If he ever saw that nitwit again

he'd knock him to kingdom come. That wasn't much use to Soraya, right now, though.

Simon set three mugs on a tray, and carried them with the cafetiere and jug of milk, Soraya's spice mix, and a small jar of honey.

'Jorge saw your typewritten manuscript in my writing room. He put two and two together.'

'You really didn't tell him?'

'I promise you. He must have seen it there while you and I were finishing dinner.'

Soraya let out a long breath.

'It's *my* fault he found out? I don't know what to do.'

'Right now, you don't need to know anything. Just drink your coffee.'

Soraya sobbed throughout the afternoon, cushioned by her sister's arms.

'You'll get through this, honey. We'll help you get through this.'

'I should never have gone to New York. If only I'd stayed here. None of this would have happened. Simon, please go back home. There's no place for you here.'

'I told you, Soraya, he saw your manuscript!'

'I don't care. I want you to leave.'

Santana looked at him pityingly. 'It's best if you go, Simon. She needs her space.'

Simon stood up, reluctantly. 'Don't let this come between us, Soraya. Please.'

And as he walked away, she didn't dare look up. Soraya didn't want to witness him leaving her life for the last time.

# Betrayal

Simon reluctantly drove away from House of Hearts, and out of Rainbow Valley; far, far away from the love of his life. And what of his heart? Heavy and numb, it plodded on as if by rote; each beat a limp struggle onwards, as if there was no point in beating anymore. If only he could understand why she let him walk away, even though she knew it was Jorge Perez behind the media storm. *If only.* Several times he hit the steering wheel as he swore. It just didn't make sense. Nothing made sense except for the fact they were irresistibly drawn to each other, and now she was letting him walk away. He replayed their last phone conversation over and over in his head. It was so obvious that they were going to find a way to be together permanently. Why else would she have encouraged him to travel all the way to her home?

Three hours out of the valley, and just an hour from the comfort of his luxurious home, the fuel-warning lamp came on and beeped five times. Simon pulled into the nearest gas station, and refuelled.

'What do you mean the card's been rejected?' Simon snapped. In no mood for faulty technology, he pulled out another bank card and passed it to the teller.

As he put the first card back into his wallet, the teller looked up helplessly and mumbled. 'Sorry, sir, this one isn't going through either. Do you have another card you could try? Or,' she stuttered, 'perhaps you have cash?'

At this point, he could feel his blood boiling. With every fibre of his being, he knew it wasn't the teller's fault. Nothing about this horrible day was her fault, but if things didn't improve instantly, she was going to bear the brunt of his anger. And by God he was angry!

'This card will work,' he assured her, passing over his American Express. he hated using credit.

The payment went through without a hitch, but he was left wondering why the two cards connected to his bank accounts weren't working. There was more than enough money readily available for not just a rainy day, but a damn typhoon. Enough money to save the city!

Collapsing onto the sofa, Simon sighed. All that driving, and for what? To be told to turn away? It just didn't make sense. If he ever saw Jorge Perez, he'd make sure the guy never got a job working in media again. The thought that one heartless person could change the course of another person's life—a *good* person's life— had him questioning everything he held valid about human nature. The familiar whistle of the kettle gave him hope: coffee. He wanted to make it black coffee, but Soraya's sweet voice in his head insisted he add cream and honey. And what the heck, he sprinkled a little cinnamon on for good measure.

Within minutes, he was logging onto his online banking, coffee in one hand, laptop mouse in the other. Available balance: $0.00. 'What the hell?'

It took about thirty seconds for Simon to register the zeros. Oh, he was used to zeros, but plenty of them, and with digits before them. Clearly the bank had made an error somewhere. Logging onto his other account, he choked on his coffee when the available balance came onto the screen: $0.00. Both accounts each had a single withdrawal for the entire balance. It had to be a technical error. Simon stood up, paced the room, and then sat back down. It was the weekend, so there was no way of actually speaking to a human if he phoned the bank.

Checking a couple of small-balance accounts, he was reassured to see that there were some funds available should he need any purchases before Monday. He had his American Express, too, but the overriding question was: *Where the hell has my money gone?*

Monday morning, nine o'clock, seemed to stretch out like a treeless desert, teasing him mercilessly, as if he were crawling on his hands and knees to a mirage.

'This is Simon Beaudin, please put me through to the branch manager. Thank you.' He read out his account numbers, impatient for an explanation. 'There's been nothing on the news about computer hitches. What's going on?'

'Mr Beaudin, the balance of both accounts was moved by electronic transfer on Saturday morning, at approximately 10am. Are you certain you didn't transfer that money?'

'I think I'd remember if I shifted that sort of cash, don't you?'

'Who else has access to your account?'

'No one!'

'No one has your passwords?'

'No one has my passwords, I can assure you.'

There were a few moments silence, before the manager spoke again.

'Mr Beaudin, I see that this used to be a joint account with Bonnie Halliwell. Does she have access to your passwords?'

'With all due respect, sir, she hasn't been in my life or sharing this account for eight years. And I can assure you that my passwords were changed when her name was taken off both accounts.'

'I don't have any answers for you right now, Mr Beaudin. I'm terribly sorry. Can I call you back in an hour? I need to speak to someone in the money-tracing team. The money from both accounts has been moved to an off-shore account. I can't see where it's gone.'

Simon fumed. *Bonnie?* Why the hell would she do that? The settlement he gave her for the three years of their de facto relationship was beyond adequate. She'd said so herself. Simon pulled out his address book. The last person he wanted to speak to was Bonnie, but he needed that money back.

'It's Simon. Simon Beaudin. Bonnie, I see you've had a little shopping spree. I have no idea how you guessed my passwords, but you need to return that money straight away. I will call the police if it's not back in my account by the end of business today.'

Simon waited for her to answer. He knew her well enough to know that within seconds she'd apologise profusely for her silly mistake. But there was no apology, and there was no denial.

'I'm busy, Simon. Can't chat right now. Sorry. Take good care of yourself.'

'I mean it, Bonnie, I'll call…'

The phone was already dead. Damn it! He redialled, but it was engaged.

Suddenly his mind raced to figure out how he could access more cash. Cash was king, next to real estate. Sure, he had plenty of the latter, but there was no telling how long it would take for any of his properties to sell in the current economy. Yes, he could extend his credit and overdraft options, but he disliked debt of any description. Simon wanted his money back, and he'd damn well drive the two hours to Bonnie's house if he had to. If she still lived there.

He'd done his best to cut her out of his life when it became abundantly clear that she had only one interest in him: his money. Simon had been generous to a fault, but always put an upper limit on what she could spend at any time. Money slipped through her hands like sands in an hourglass, but she never took notice. Bonnie knew there was always plenty more, and always stretched her shopping expenses. Every single time. Simon grew weary of it, and of her total lack of respect for his income.

*Tring, tring. Tring, tring.*

Simon nearly jumped out of his skin. 'Simon Beaudin.' His voice was curt. He was in no mood for games.

'Les King, branch manager. I'm sorry Mr Beaudin. We're unable to trace the money, other than to say it's offshore. You do have the insurance on those accounts, so we can put some funds in there today, but as for the balance, that's out of our hands. I can recommend a forensic accountant to look into this. Would you like his number?'

'Yes, of course.' He scribbled down the details, and made the call.

'Mr Beaudin, change your passwords straight away.'

Simon felt like a fifteen-year-old boy being hauled into the headmaster's office, then took a few deep breaths before making his next call.

'No, I can't *prove* it was Bonnie Halliwell. The passwords were an exact match. I don't keep written records of my passwords anywhere, just in my memory. She's the only person in the world who knows me well enough to be able to come close to figuring them out. And even then, they were a long shot. Or so I thought.'

The accountant didn't make any promises, other than to say it was at the top of his list. He warned Simon that it could take months to trace the money, and even then, there was no guarantee they could get it back.

Simon let the words sink in slowly, as he sipped a glass of Irish whiskey. He was tired. So tired. He rubbed his eyes, fighting off exhaustion. The next call on his list was to his accountant.

'Jesus, that's rough. Look, Simon, you know the financial world better than anyone. Without that cash, you're in a tight spot. You're still a very wealthy man, you always will be, but you can't sell the sort of properties you own overnight. They could take months, maybe years. Your best bet is to hope the forensic accountant can do a quick trace. I can shift some funds from one of your portfolios, but your lifestyle will have to change dramatically if you can't get this sorted. I'm really sorry.'

This had to be one of the worst weeks of his life, and both events involved women. One bad, and one good. He let out a sarcastic laugh. Bonnie and Soraya couldn't have been more different from each other. One, conniving. The other, self-sufficient and…gorgeous. Oh God how he missed her! How had things come to this point?

Simon took a shower, then sat down on the sofa to plan his next move. The offending newspaper with the article exposing Soraya as Ashley Starr sat there, a silent witness to his agony. Ironic, isn't it, he thought, that 'the man of money' has none. Not a single cent. How was that possible?

Despite his fury, he couldn't help laugh. What

would Soraya make of his heart now? It certainly wasn't made of money this afternoon.

His thoughts turned to Bonnie. Why, after all these years, did she steal his money? What could have prompted such an attack on him? The answer was staring at him, but it took at least five minutes for Simon to connect the dots: she'd read the article about Soraya and seen her relationship to Simon mentioned. Jealous?

*But it's been years!*

Simon thought of his parting conversation with Bonnie, on the day she moved out. On the day he *forced* her to move out. The day he couldn't bear to look at her any longer.

'Don't you ever fall in love with anyone, or I'll make you pay!' She spat the words, after a few gins too many, as she tumbled into the back seat of a cab.

He couldn't understand her possessiveness then, and he couldn't understand it now. Bonnie had lost her job as a high-flying TV producer just a month before he called an end to their relationship, and he was beyond generous in helping her establish a new life. The truth was, he'd have paid her double just to be free of her. Simon learnt his lesson the hard way: don't drink too much if you bring a woman back to your penthouse for the night. And keep your wits about you if she happens to love the taste of money. Simon had no excuses for her moving in with him virtually straight away, other than that he'd been on a career high, and his ego had got the better of him. Truth was, he loved the taste of money, and he rather enjoyed the fact that women dropped at his feet.

Bonnie Halliwell had been a steep learning curve, but he thought he'd learned his lesson well. But right now, he felt like his testicles were in a vice! Eight years on, and she was still taking him for a ride! He prayed the forensic money search wouldn't take too long.

Simon phoned the police to report the theft. He was staggered to hear that there was little they could do until they had confirmation from the bank or the forensic accountant about the whereabouts of the funds.

'Unless you have firm proof, Mr Beaudin, our hands are tied.'

'Unbelievable!' he shouted as he slammed the phone down. 'Un-bloody-believable!'

The clock radio mocked him: 3am. Sleep was never going to come easily. How could it, when his life had just been turned upside down? He got up, his naked body reflecting the moonlight as he strode around the lounge, and stopped by the phone. Soraya. He needed to hear her voice. It would be a balm to the turbulent forces careening into his identity. Who was he without his hard-earned cash? The last thing he wanted—hell, the last thing he needed—was to have an identity crisis. He could hear her soft words: *there's more to life than money, Simon.*

In the morning, he'd start selling off bonds and shares.

In the morning, he'd phone Soraya.

When morning arrived, however, he stood by the phone for an hour. Simon reached for it several times, then turned away, his fingers shaking. She'd made it clear that she didn't want him. Soraya was going through her own identity crisis, anyway. Perhaps she wouldn't be nearly as sympathetic as he'd hoped. More importantly, he'd have to explain how someone—not just anyone, but someone he'd failed to declare: *a de facto lover*—had correctly guessed not one password, but two. That they happened to be the same passwords were, to Simon's mind, a minor detail. He cursed himself for singing the old ABBA song every morning in the shower: *Money, Money, Money.* Perhaps, to Bonnie, it hadn't been that hard to guess at all.

Despite his splitting headache, Simon booked an appointment with his investment broker. It was time to start reeling in the cash. If there was any hope in the world of Soraya coming back into his life, he wanted it to be in the style and comfort she had come to expect when she was with him. Nothing less would do. He'd fight tooth and nail to find that cash, and he'd do it because of one woman: Soraya. She deserved to share in every cent of his hard-earned fortune.

# Vulnerable

The next few weeks passed in a haze. Soraya would wake each morning to start sifting the ingredients for gingerbread hearts, and then realise she had no customers to give them to. She found herself aching for Simon's arms, and wishing he was by her side. Not once had he emailed or phoned. She shouldn't have been surprised. After all, she'd made it perfectly clear that he was not welcome in her life.

Christmas was just days away. This would normally be one of her busiest times in the shop, even when there were snowdrifts. And oh how she loved the busyness: a mask to hide the pain of December 24th which always loomed large during the so-called festive season.

It wasn't that she had writer's block, but she struggled to put words on the page. Somehow the idea of love seemed meaningless. All these years of offering hope and sensuality to millions of women around the world, when what she really wanted was to have all these things for herself! And she wanted them with Simon. Simon Beaudin. She was no longer living in the past. Without even being aware of it, she had begun healing from her lost loves. Simon had helped her to do that. Every time he touched her, she let go of a deep ache. It was Simon who'd shown her that the heart was big enough to keep on loving. It might not have been his intention, but he was a master at the craft of loving her into full being. Or, more accurately, loving Soraya Juniper. The truth was: everything about Soraya Juniper was easy to love.

Soraya had this day circled on her calendar for six longs weeks: plaster cast removed. She had lived a lifetime since the day she met Simon Beaudin. And had her life turned upside down!

Santana drove her to the hospital, and stayed by her side.

'How does it feel to be a free woman?' she laughed, as they left the front of the building.

'Free? I've never felt more imprisoned in my life,' she said, sadness trickling down her cheeks.

'You could just phone him, you know?' she said tenderly, reaching for her twin sister's hand.

'What are you talking about?'

'Simon's not going to make the first move. You have to call him. You pushed him away. There's no way he can read your mind, Soraya. If you want him, call him. Go there, if you have to. Don't let him walk away. This man is right for you.'

'All men are the same!'

'They're not, and you know it. Soraya, come on, you're the Queen of Love. Why give it to everyone else but deny yourself? Life's too short. And frankly, men like Simon are pretty rare.'

'We're so different! We're not compatible!'

'What a load of rubbish. I've seen you two together. That man is so smitten with you I'm amazed he even walked away. And remember, he fell for you before he knew anything about Ashley Starr.'

'I can't do this, San. I can't get hurt again.'

'He is not going to hurt you. He's not like that. Why do you think he's still a bachelor? The man knows pain. But he also knows what it looks like to have the right one come along.'

'How do you know? What's he said to you?'

'It's what he hasn't said. Look Soraya, no man and no situation can ever hurt you as much as you hurt

177

yourself. Stop reliving the traumatic events of your life, and grab this guy with both hands. Before it's too late. You can't expect him to wait forever, even if he does think you're the right one.'

Soraya paced her lounge room. Was Santana right? Should she just go and profess her undying love to Simon? She picked up her cellphone, scrolled down the address book until she reached S.

S for serendipity.

S for snowstorm.

S for sensual.

S for sexuality.

S for Simon.

Her fingers were shaking.

'Simon,' she texted, 'meet me at your yacht at 3pm tomorrow. Soraya.' Her breathing became rapid. Oh God, she said to herself, what have I done? There's no turning back now. There's nothing to stop us being together.

At sunrise the next day, she packed a suitcase, and got into her car. It wouldn't start. Not surprising, really, given she'd not driven in it for almost two months and the weather was icy cold. After a frustrating two hours waiting for the roadside rescue, she was finally on her way to New York. Finally on her way to meet the love of her life.

At several intersections she stopped, almost ready to turn around and go home. Too much time had passed, she told herself. He hadn't been in touch. Maybe he'd moved on? Maybe she really was just a passing fling to him? Maybe it was just a brief affair and she was reading too much into it?

Something—she didn't know what—made her drive on.

At 2.30pm, she found the marina car park, and got out. Although she was rugged up against the bitter Winter winds, she pulled her collar up higher around her neck. A yacht? What was she thinking! Right now, she needed a furnace to warm her up. There was only a half an hour left till he arrived. What was she doing walking along the marina?

And there he was. Early. Standing on the deck of *My Darling*, a tentative look on his face. Why wasn't he smiling? Was he here against his will? Perhaps this was a stupid idea. Maybe she had left reconciliation too late?

She found herself dumbstruck as she edged nearer. If only he'd smile, at least it would show that he was glad to see her.

'I wanted to try out your Jacuzzi,' she said softly, pointing to her plasterless leg.

'Would you like some company?' he asked, stepping closer to her and reaching his hand out as she stepped on board.

'I would.'

'Max is making us a meal. It'll be at least a couple of hours. That should give us plenty of time.'

'Have you got time?' she asked, her eyes never leaving his.

'For you? I've got all the time in the world. I will always have all the time in the world for you, Soraya. Always.'

Snowflakes fell onto their naked shoulders as they sat beneath the steamy water of the intimate, oasis-like Jacuzzi. Whatever troubles had plagued them, now melted away with the powerful jets of water.

'I'm curious about something,' Simon said, kissing her neck.

'What's that?' she asked, enjoying how good it felt to be lying against his chest and safe in his arms once again.

'That cheating ex-lover. The one whose heart you ate? What did he do?'

'Turns out he was already married.'

'Christ! And you had no idea?'

'None at all. I was still grieving for Liam so needed plenty of time on my own, even though two years had passed. Well, he never argued with that, and was quite happy with our arrangement. He lived over an hour away, so it was pretty unlikely I'd ever find out until the relationship got serious. But, for me, it was serious. My heart had already been broken, and every day was an exercise in willpower. I happened to be in his town picking up some supplies, when I drove by the playground and smiled at the happy family by the swings. It didn't register straight away, seeing him with a toddler on his shoulders and pushing a young child on the swing. It was out of context.'

'I'm so sorry. No wonder you're wary of relationships. You didn't deserve that.'

'No, I didn't. I felt like he was cheating on me, even though it was his wife he was actually cheating on. I haven't dated anyone since.'

'Until now.'

She turned around and smiled. 'Until now.'

'One of the hardest things about being in a

relationship is the level of vulnerability that's required to be truly intimate. Emotionally intimate,' he said, holding her closer. 'That connection, compassion and courage has to come from a place so deep within that many of us can't find it because we're so disconnected. When I said to you that I hadn't found anyone I wanted to invest in, what I meant was that I hadn't found anyone before I met you, Soraya. I've been burnt before, not by love, but by being with someone who wasn't right for me. I decided that I'd rather be on my own than be in a half-hearted relationship. I didn't believe in love.'

She closed her eyes and listen to his words. Words and sentiments she'd ached to hear from the day he walked into her pretty little shop. Words that would have seemed impossible from a hard-nosed financial journalist.

Soraya thought about words, and how her lucrative career had relied on her finding just the right ones. And it dawned on her that, despite her prolific output, she'd not once expressed the template of love and loving as eloquently as Simon just had. In fact, she realised, she'd spent so much of her time thinking they were mismatched; when all along he knew her better than anyone ever had; loved her more than any man ever could. Her heart squeezed tight, as he kissed her neck, and held her hand.

'What are you thinking about, Soraya? You've gone all quiet.'

'Just how lucky I am. How incredibly blessed I am.'

'No, darling. I'm the lucky one. I nearly didn't follow Gemma's suggestion. If I hadn't have gone to see you, my life would be so much poorer.'

'Have you ever loved another woman, Simon?'

'I have cared for other women.'

'Did your heart break? Is that why you didn't settle down?'

He laughed. 'All your questions, Soraya.' Simon sighed, and then turned her around so they were facing each other. 'My heart didn't break, no. And that was the problem. I knew that I needed a woman who was so incredible that if she walked away from me I'd never be the same again. That didn't happen until the day I met you. My heart broke the morning I upset you over the coffee. That's when I knew you were the one for me, even though I kept trying to deny it. I simply couldn't bear to see the sadness on your face. I never wanted to see you upset again.'

'Really? Over a cup of coffee?'

'Yes, my love.'

'You know it was decaff, right?' she laughed.

Simon let out a hearty laugh, and leaned forward to kiss her. 'And what did you hope to achieve by giving me decaff?'

'To put you in country-town time. You were so buzzed up from New York life that it disturbed the ambience of House of Hearts.'

'Are you sure it wasn't your pulse I was disturbing?'

'Oh, you disturbed my pulse alright!'

Sometime later, when fingertips became prune-like, Simon suggested they leave the Jacuzzi and take a quick shower before dinner.

Under the full head of steam, he held her close. 'God, I've missed you! I don't ever want to be apart from you again. Are we clear on that?'

'Simon?'

'Yes?'

'There's something you should know.'

Simon's heart pounded. Whatever it was, he wasn't sure he wanted to know. Of course she could move to New York. Hell, he'd even move to the valley or Toledo, if it came to it. The important thing was that they were together. Now. Always. They could even live on the yacht if he had to sell the penthouse.

'I never did eat his heart. I'm vegetarian.' They both laughed, and in seconds he hoisted her up against the tiles, securing her with his hips.

Soraya winced at the cool marble tiles pressed against her bottom, but Simon soon warmed her up. Already she was limp, as his kisses coaxed her towards him. The steamy heat from the shower spray was no match for the temperatures they were generating.

'I want to hold you here forever, Soraya, in front of me. I never want to stop looking at your beautiful face,' he said, his words barely a whisper. His hands held her hips securely, but he was desperate to feel her, all of her. For a moment, he was worried she must have been cold, but his body told him otherwise. She was hot. Smokin' hot. Steamy, in fact.

Simon was entranced by how flexible her legs were, and that she was able to wrap them around his waist so easily.

As if reading his mind, she whispered, 'Years of yoga!'

'Don't ever give up, then,' he laughed

Whatever was in her words, it didn't come close to matching the look on her face. It wasn't desperation, but surrender. A beautiful mermaid seducing him beneath a waterfall of heat and sensuality. If he hadn't already fallen in love with Soraya Juniper, he most certainly would have. She was offering herself up on a portal of sublime sexuality and potent sensuality.

'I want to become one with you, in every sense of the word. Don't leave me. I don't want anything to come between us, not now, not ever,' she whispered, spiralling closer to ecstasy, and she started heading to that last tip of the mountain, higher, higher, higher; each moment seeming like a never-ending struggle to reach the summit: the promise of exquisite treasure and pleasure. And there, right there, as she spun on top of the world, feeling like anything—*absolutely anything in the world*—was possible, Soraya Juniper gave her heart and body to the love of her life.

Slowly, they came down from the tiers of rapture, one octave at a time. It was a journey that they'd make many, many times in the years ahead, they were sure of it, but the view and terrain would always bring something new to their lives. One thing Simon was clear about: there wasn't anyone else in the world he would have preferred for his travelling companion. For richer, or for poorer.

Neither of them had ever had a shower quite like it before. At some point, sated on the shower floor, they managed to untangle themselves from each other and find the soap. She looked up at him from beneath her wet hair, and smiled. 'Again?'

At eight o'clock, they both agreed it was time for dinner. All that exercise and no food? Ridiculous! Simon dressed in a tuxedo. He'd waited so long for this night. Everything had to be perfect. When they danced later on the deck, he wanted it to be in style. Soraya was still doing her makeup, her hair wrapped in a towel, when he left the bedroom.

'I'll see you up on the deck when you're ready,' he said, then kissed her shoulder. Soraya smiled back at him, her reflection in the mirror an image he wanted to preserve forever.

Dressed in a holly-red crushed-velvet ballgown, Soraya stepped onto the covered dining area of the deck. She'd taken a lot of care choosing this dress. In her mind, she wanted to be a fairy princess; someone the prince couldn't refuse. Tonight she was Cinderella.

'You look stunning,' he whispered, the words catching in his throat. 'Absolutely stunning. Come here,' Simon said, watching the white snowflakes outside the window contrast against the deep red of her dress.

Soraya almost felt as if she was looking down on her life as she stepped towards Simon, with Barbra Streisand on the stereo singing *What Are You Doing the Rest Of Your Life?* The nightlights of New York twinkled in the background. The aroma of Max's creations wafted out from the kitchen. The pangs in her stomach told her one thing: she was hungry. Hungry for life! There was no going back now. Soraya was ready for more. She was ready for everything.

'You look pretty amazing yourself,' she smiled. 'And I can smell Chanel Egoiste,' she laughed.

'Just for you,' he smiled, reaching for her hand. 'Everything I do is for you.'

Simon pulled back a dining chair, and allowed Soraya to be seated.

They shared a comfortable silence for a few minutes, just grateful to be with each other. It was all a bit surreal.

'This is a beautiful meal,' Soraya said, as the

waiter placed a linen napkin across her lap. He lifted her entrée from a silver tray: green-curry soup with delicate flavours of lemongrass, ginger, coriander and coconut.

'Only the best for you,' Simon said.

'There's something about this evening,' she said. 'I can't put it into words, but it just feels...'

'Meaningful?'

'Yes, and memorable. I don't want to ever forget sitting here with you.'

'I suspect you won't,' he smiled.

They didn't speak much for the next twenty minutes. Mostly, they stared into each other's eyes, smiling and laughing, unable to comprehend the rich gifts life had brought them.

All the money in the world couldn't bring lovers together like this. It required the hand of something much greater: destiny.

The main meal was served: crisp-fried cake of mushrooms and chestnuts on garlic-butter spinach with a tarragon cream sauce served with seasonal vegetables.

Simon couldn't wait any longer, and pulled something out of his pocket. 'I know Christmas is a sore spot for you, and I can't do anything to change your past, but I'm hoping I can make your future brighter; make it something that excites you. I want you to look forward to every Christmas, with me; with our children.'

'What is it?' Soraya asked, surprised by his gift giving. The look of love in his eyes as he smiled was worth more than all the money in the world. She hoped he knew that. Soraya wanted this moment to last forever. Did he just say *our children*?

'Is this a special playlist you've made?' she asked

186

when the next song played: *Hopeless Romantic* by Billy Vera.

'Might have,' he laughed.

With trembling fingers, she opened the silver wrapping paper and ribbon, and held the navy-blue velvet box. Was it a ring? Her heart skipped a beat. Surely not? This was too soon. Way too soon. Wasn't it? When you have 'I've known you forever' at first sight, is there such a thing as too soon? What could it be?

'Open it,' he urged. What if she said no? What if she wasn't ready for such a commitment? What if she didn't want to invest in *him*? It wasn't a thought he could bear. Not now. Not when they'd come this far. There'd been too many hurdles for her to walk away now.

'Oh Simon, it's gorgeous!' she said, swooning as her trembling fingers outlined the antique-silver heart-shaped locket. 'This is stunning!' She traced over the engraved pattern on the front.

'It was my grandmother's locket. My grandfather gave it to her instead of an engagement ring. He said anyone could wear a ring, but only someone who had stolen his heart could wear a locket like this.'

Tears slipped from Soraya's eyes. She didn't dare open it. The thought of it not having their photos inside was too much. One day she'd put them in there, though. Her heart was overwhelmed with joy.

'Open the locket,' Simon said, smiling as he tried to steady her shaking hands. And then he realised his hands were shaking too. Of course they were. This was the most important moment of his life.

Soraya smiled at the sight of Simon's face embedded into one side of the heart, and her photo on the other side.

'Simon.' She cried. 'Are you...are you proposing to me?'

'Merry Christmas, my darling. I love you so much. I love you with all my heart. And, believe me, there's a huge heart inside me filled to the brim with nothing but you. You're the best thing that's ever happened in my life. Everything that I thought was so important, so indicative of success, pales into insignificance unless you're part of my world.'

Simon wiped the tears trickling down her face.

'My darling, I only have one wish for you.'

'What is that?' she sniffed, realising her greatest dreams had come true: that her soulmate had finally found her; that Simon Beaudin loved her as much as she loved him.

'That you always think of me as *third time lucky*.'

'Always,' she cried, sitting on his lap and wrapping her arms around him. 'Always!'

## ~ THE END ~

# Soraya's Gingerbread Love Hearts

½ teaspoon cinnamon
½ teaspoon ground cloves
½ teaspoon nutmeg
3 teaspoons ground ginger
¼ cup blackstrap molasses
1 cup brown sugar
¼ cup soya or rice or dairy milk
½ teaspoon sea salt
3/4 cup raw brown sugar or maple syrup
1/3 cup light olive or sunflower oil
2 cups of all-purpose flour (gluten-free works fine)
½ teaspoon baking powder
½ teaspoon baking soda (bicarbonate of soda)
½ teaspoon organic lemon zest

*cup = 250 grams
* use a measuring teaspoon

Whisk the sugar and oil, then add the lemon zest, milk and molasses. Stir in the sifted dry ingredients. When a dough forms, place in the fridge for at least an hour. You can leave it for a day or two if you like. This will really allow the spices to infuse the other ingredients. When ready to bake, preheat the oven to 160C. Roll the dough out onto a floured board, and cut your gingerbread hearts out with your heart-shaped cutter. Carefully place on a baking tray, and bake for eight minutes. When cooked, leave them on the tray for a few minutes before placing on a cooling rack.

# Novels by Veronika Robinson

Mosaic
Bluey's Café

*The Gypsy Moon Trilogy*
Sisters of the Silver Moon
Behind Closed Doors
Flowers in Her Hair

*Sweet Cinnamon Romance*
Love at the Treble Clef Café
Love in a Scottish Storm
On the Wings of Love
Recipe for Love
House of Hearts

*Moonlight and Motif*
*(magical realism novels publishing in 2023)*
The Button Tin
The Soapmaker
The Irish Dollmaker

For a list of the author's non-fiction titles, visit
www.veronikarobinson.com

## *Review Me*

As an indie author, it would mean the world
to me if you left a review of this book on
Amazon or your chosen online retailer. Thank
you so much! May happiness be with you
always. Veronika x

# **About the Artist:** Heidi Harbers

Happiest when she's brightening up the world, whether it's decorating a room, painting a mural, growing a garden, feeding her chickens avocados, or organising fun events in her village, creativity is at the heart of Heidi's life.

As a pub landlady, and former restaurant owner, she has cooked for thousands of people across the years, serving up delicious meals, both traditional and unusual. When not cooking, Heidi's flare for transforming bare walls into canvases for her community to enjoy has earned her a wonderful reputation.

Australian born and raised, Heidi has travelled the world; and for many years has called England home. Born under the zodiac sign of Libra, the lovers, it is only natural that her art has found a home on the covers of romance novels.

*Only when the last river has been poisoned, and the last fish has been caught,*
*will we realise we cannot eat money.*
~ Cree Indian proverb.